GILGAMESH

RETOLD BY
GERALDINE McCAUGHREAN

ILLUSTRATED BY
DAVID PARKINS

"He walked through darkness, and so glimpsed the light."

EERDMANS BOOKS FOR YOUNG READERS
Grand Rapids, Michigan • Cambridge, U.K.

The Epic of Gilgamesh is the oldest recorded story in the world. It was originally carved on twelve stone tablets which, over thousands of years, were smashed into thousands of shards. Even now, for all the painstaking work of restoration, different scholars place the events of the story in different orders, and some episodes are still lost.

Gilgamesh is thought to have been a real king reigning some time between 3200 BC and 2700 BC over the Sumerian city of Uruk, in Mesopotamia (now Iraq). He led expeditions into neighboring territories, to fetch back timber for his grand building projects.

The story of the Flood—several floods devastated the region —found its way into other cultures, ultimately into the Bible, undergoing changes according to the religion of the teller.

The work of archaeology is incomplete; some of the tile fragments still baffle interpreters. This version is a free adaptation from a variety of translations.

CONTENTS

1 Heaven Sent

Gilgamesh dreamed that a meteor crashed to earth at his feet.

Everyone came running from their houses, pointing, excitable. They crowded round the meteor marveling at the hugeness of it, the harm it might have done if it had fallen on a building, on a child. They pushed at it, but twelve men together could not so much as budge it.

In his dream, Gilgamesh put a strip of leather round the rock and, resting the strap across his forehead, strained to lift it. The crowd fell back in awe. Though it weighed more than a hundred sacks of grain, Gilgamesh lifted the meteor clear of the ground and, hands braced on his knees, staggered with it to his mother. But just as he arrived at her door, he woke.

So he carried her the dream, instead. It weighed almost as heavy on his thoughts as the meteor had on his forehead, and he had great difficulty explaining the passion he had felt towards this . . . this . . . rock. It sounded so foolish.

His mother, Ninsun, did not laugh. She did not make light of his dark dream. "The gods are sending you a wife, perhaps, or a visitor—some foreign king or sage. Someone of great importance."

"This is not the first time," he admitted. "I dreamt another dream."

"Tell me," said Ninsun.

"I dreamed I was walking through the streets of Uruk, and I saw an axe lying on the ground. It was beautiful, mother! I had to pick it up. I had to own it! So I slipped it through my belt and wore it by my side, and I was so pleased to have it, I can't begin to say . . ." He stopped short. It sounded so footling.

But his mother did not laugh. "Ah! Now I see. It's someone much more important than a king or a sage or a wife. The gods are sending you a *friend*!"

Gilgamesh frowned. He did not know what to make of his mother's words, what to think about the prospect of a friend. He had seen rocks before, and axes. But even in a dream, he had never had such a thing as a friend. The idea was as strange to him as a piece of heaven breaking free and falling to earth.

Hunter threw down his bundle of tools in disgust. He squatted down and cupped a drink from the waterhole with both hands, then slapped the water so hard that a dozen little fish skittered out of sight. Three days, and he had not caught a single animal! Someone had slashed his nets, smashed his snares, filled in the pits he had dug. But who? And why?

The fish regrouped. Hunter pulled a big waterside leaf over him to keep off the sun. Otherwise he would never have seen the creature come down to drink.

The sight made all the hairs stand up on his neck. The creature came down to the water, walking on the balls of his long feet, on the knuckles of his large hands. His entire body, but for the palms of his hands, the inside crooks of his arms and the hollows of his eyes were matted with hair. But this was no bear or cat. He bent his head down to sip directly from the water, but this was no antelope or hog. He had a mane of long wiry hair, but this was no lion. This was a *man*.

Hunter waited, motionless, for the beast to finish drinking and to stalk away. He held so still that the fish nibbled his toes. He held still while ants crawled up his arms and the flies settled on him in clouds. Not until the creature had loped away, head up, the water glistening on his pelt, did Hunter snatch up his tools and run.

Afterwards, he wondered if he had imagined it: the sun too hot on his head, the light too bright on the water. Next day, he had more to worry him than imaginary beasts. Once again, his traps were all smashed, his pits all filled up. Once again he found himself cooling his anger at the waterhole. He splashed his face; he skimmed an angry stone.

The stone bounced six, seven times, then a fist closed over it, and the man-beast was looking back at him across the lake, with sharp, dark eyes, teeth bared. Hunter fled for his life.

"It was there again, father! I saw it!" he gasped as he stumbled into camp. "Bigger than a lion! Stronger than a bull! I've never seen a man like him, father! He's the one who's been cutting my nets and smashing my traps and filling in my pits! With him out there, I'll never catch another beast!"

His father blinked his blind old eyes and said, "King Gilgamesh has more wisdom than most. Go to Uruk, son, and ask the mighty Gilgamesh what to do."

Hunter did not hesitate. He ran and ran, already happier and more hopeful. The name of Uruk was full of magic to him: a place he had never been, but a place famous throughout the world for its wonder. Long before the strip of gold on the horizon resolved itself into bricks and buttresses, Hunter knew it was the shining wall of Uruk, curving out of the plain like a wave breaking. Before he could clearly see patterns on the strip of gold, he knew they were the carved memorials of great men.

"Where can I find Gilgamesh the King!" he panted, resting his hands on his knees.

The men at the gate scowled at him. The women by the well turned aside their eyes. He might as well have named the monster Huwawa.

So Hunter headed for the largest palace, the tallest tower, and asked there for Gilgamesh.

"Why?" asked the men at the door. "Go away from here, huntsman. You were better off in the wilderness."

"Why?" asked Hunter, gazing around him in wonder at the glazed tiles, the ivory carvings, the great glossy teak bowls of flower petals, the host of servants silent as shadows. "What more wonderful place on earth is there than Uruk?"

"None," replied the usher who led him to the King's audience chamber. "If it weren't for its King. I do not know what troubles bring you to Uruk, young man. None so great as ours, I'll be bound. For what greater burden can a city bear than Gilgamesh?" And the word fell from his mouth with the wriggle and hiss of a serpent: *Gilgamesh.*

"Gilgamesh?" Hunter was astounded. "But he's famous! Never loses a battle! Beautiful like a god! Everyone says . . . !"

"Hmmm," said the usher, and the look on his face admitted that all of those things were true.

"What, then? Is he a despot? A tyrant?"

The usher breathed a sigh of unspeakable weariness. "He has worn us down like a river flowing through a gorge. Like a waterfall splashing on to rocks. So much life, so much energy. He makes perpetual war, you know? He spends our sons like so many arrows in his quiver. And for what? For the excitement of a battle charge. He is forever building new towers. For what? For the sake of touching the sky. You see the wall that surrounds Uruk? Who do you think toiled under the sun to drag the stones?

We call on the gods to spare us, but on and on runs Gilgamesh, with us for the soles of his sandals!"

The usher showed Hunter into the great hall of Gilgamesh the Mighty. And there Hunter saw him: an exceptionally tall young man standing on the sill of the great window, watching the building work in progress outside.

He paced incessantly up and down, tossing out orders like lava bombs from a volcano. "That stone is orange, not gold! That door does not hang true! Curse Huwawa! If it weren't for him, I would build in cedarwood! Fetch up another team of oxen!" He was outrageously handsome, with huge dark eyes and springy short black hair. The tissue of his linen skirt was so fine that his legs showed through quite plainly—a runner's legs. His skin gleamed with almond oil, and he smelt of the bathhouse and of nutmeg. His belt was gold wire, his collar of lapis lazuli, and when he turned his great eyes on Hunter, it was as if Enlil the Creator had paused in shaping the world to watch a hovering bee.

It also seemed to Hunter that the King had been expecting someone else. A pang of disappointment crossed the handsome face at seeing a mere trapper.

9

"O mighty king, your wisdom is . . . talked of all over," said Hunter awkwardly. Then he blurted out his story of the Wild Man.

The King listened with only half an ear, still watching the building work from the window. His feet were never still; he looked like a man treading water. When Hunter fell silent, Gilgamesh turned and smiled the most fleeting of smiles. "Go and find the prettiest dancing girl in Uruk, and take her with you to the drinking place. Use her beauty to lure the Wild Man out of the wilderness. Have her *tame* him. That is my advice."

And having given his advice, Gilgamesh's interest was gone. He was bored again, and restless. But he called out, as Hunter backed through the heavy door hanging, "Tell me . . . ! Did you meet anyone on the road? Someone on his way here? Someone . . . like me?"

"There is no one like Gilgamesh," said Hunter, and clambered backwards through the curtain as fast as it would let him.

2 Tamed by a Kiss

Enkidu was formed out of clay. Aruru, goddess of beginnings, dipped dawn fingers into the sea and pinched off a knob of earth, smoothing it into the shape of a man. And that was Enkidu.

But the clay she used was full of tree bark, leaf mold, broken snail shells and seed husks, so that the man she made was shaggy and rough, with a pelt of matted hair and a bark-brown face.

When he opened his nut-brown eyes, he found himself among animals. The wild ass would stand still while he drank her milk, the birds sing in answer to his whistle, the wild dogs fawn sooner than bite him, but Enkidu did not know if he was ass or dog or bird.

Whenever he found traps or nets or pits left by hunters, Enkidu spoiled them, because he thought of the animals as his family. But the day he saw Hunter crouching by the waterhole, he felt more puzzlement than hostility. Here was a beast like him—a small, scrawny version of the reflection Enkidu saw when he lay down to drink from the pool.

Still, Enkidu's brain was made from clay, and after the trapper ran away and his smell faded from the waterhole, Enkidu forgot him.

Then suddenly one day, there came an altogether different smell. As sweet as wild honey, it made the long hairs stir on Enkidu's skin. He walked fast, then faster, breaking into a loping run. The smell was like hunger and thirst, hot and cold all rolled together into a craving.

The woman was sitting cross-legged on a blanket, her eyes trailing butterflies through the sunlit trees. At the sight of Enkidu, she raised one arm, waved one hand. She was totally, goldenly, shell-smoothly naked.

For hour after hour, there she sat, fanning herself with a large leaf, or plaiting her long black hair. Closer and closer he sidled, bristling with uneasiness, brim-full of strange new appetites. The woman reached out a hand, curling a single finger, beckoning.

At last, Enkidu put down his head . . . and charged.

13

Arms and legs outstretched, he hurled himself, like a boulder on to an egg.

But she did not break.

And she would not fight. Instead, she curled her arms around his neck and pressed her mouth against his. "Hello," she said.

His arms and legs turned to water. His strength ebbed away like water on sand. All his instincts had been right: here was a snare, an ambush, a trap, a pit into which he had fallen. And yet Enkidu did not care. It was a sweet trap, a soft pit, a silken snare.

"I am Hatti. The trapper brought me all the way from Uruk. Have you ever seen Uruk, Wild Man? It is one of the seven cities of the plain. Once upon a time, seven wise men founded seven cities and taught the people how to pray, how to worship, how to make verses and paint and sing and write. Uruk is called 'the City of Great Streets.' In the mornings, a drum summons the men to work. You should see the robes the great men wear! In Uruk the vines grow like hair over the roofs of the houses, and the flower

sellers move about bright as hummingbirds; the women play with their little children under the shady trees, and there is always a sound of water from the wells. The river winds by, and washed clothes blow about in the trees on the riverside . . ."

As she talked, she plucked the burrs from his woolly skin and teased the matted knots out of his waist-length hair. Every time he shaped his mouth into a howl or a snarl, she pressed her lips to his.

"Come with me to the camp of the shepherds, and meet more men like yourself. Eat roast meat, white bread. Life is good among friends: the warmth of the campfire at night, the smell of baking in the mornings . . ." Her voice was musical and her words fell like rain on his brain of clay. She gave him wine, too, pouring it into his mouth along with kisses.

After seven days, the wind brought him the scent of the hills. Throwing her aside, he leapt to his feet and ran—back into the hills, his clay brain slippery with wine, his head a-rattle with words. He ran to find the wild ass, for a drink of her milk. But the asses scattered. The gazelle sprang away from him in huge arcing bounds. The wild dogs growled and the birds rose into the sky like ash from fire. He was no longer one of their kind. He had on him the smell of perfume and sweet oil and wine. Confused, alone, he roamed about, shouting some of the strange words he had heard on the woman's lips: *Jugglers! Templetop! Lugulbanda! Berry-juice! Gilgamesh!* And his roaring took him back to the drinking place. Still Hatti sat on her blanket, legs crossed, hands on her ankles. She beckoned to him, and this time he understood when she said, "Come, Enkidu, and let me show you the world of men."

Hunter was delighted at what Hatti had achieved. He could see at once that Enkidu was no longer a beast to fear. There would be no more broken traps or torn nets.

Hunter and the shepherds laughed to see how the ignorant brute called Enkidu could not even drink from a cup—did not know what to do with a loaf of bread or a dish of lentils!

15

But Hatti did not laugh. She sat beside Enkidu, her torrent of black hair breaking over his bent knee, showing him how to use a knife, how to refill a cup.

The shepherds stopped laughing when they saw him cram down seven loaves and drain the last of their wine. "Your food is good," said Enkidu finishing another loaf of bread. "What must I do to sit at your fireside another day?"

Hunter gasped. Hatti had taught the Wild Man to speak! "These shepherds take turns at night to keep watch, guarding the sheep from lions and wolves."

"No longer!" declared Enkidu. "I shall keep watch all night, and by day I shall kill lions. I sleep little."

The shepherds looked at one another in delight. The Protector of Animals had become the Protector of Flocks.

Enkidu, having lost one family in the uplands, had found another on the plains. He was happy, in a restless, waiting way.

One evening, at the fireside, Hatti said, "I should go back to Uruk. I'm a dancing girl. My place is in the City of Streets."

"Poor you," said the shepherds with genuine sympathy.

"Ah, now, Gilgamesh may be a trial to his people," argued Hunter, "but it was his genius that tamed Enkidu."

"Who is this Gilgamesh?" said Enkidu, bridling a little.

"A tyrant and a marvel, so they say."

"A blessing and a curse, I heard."

"A dream and a nightmare."

So Enkidu learned of King Gilgamesh of Uruk, who had worn down his people like water falling on a rock, who had spent them in wars like so many arrows, who exhausted them with his boundless energy. The Wild Man flared into a rage at what they told him. "Is that any way for a father of his people to behave? I shall go to Uruk and challenge this Gilgamesh!" He leapt to his feet. "This demon must not be allowed to trample the hearts of his own people! Soft-palmed, sponge-bellied city sluggard! I shall pound him into clay!"

King Gilgamesh was contemplating marriage. Every day he shut himself up in the Temple of Ishtar, goddess of Love, and the people outside could hear the slap of his sandals on the pavement. The city swarmed with panic. Rumor had it that the King would marry the terrible Ishtar herself!

Then a new stir swirled through the market place. The crowds parted for a new face: a man almost as alarming as Gilgamesh in his size and the spread of his shoulders. Hatti, the pretty little dancing girl, was with him. The crowd murmured and gasped.

"He is the size of Gilgamesh!"

"Shorter."

"Yes, but thicker set!"

"A Wild Man, bred up with the lions!"

Gilgamesh came out of the temple and turned towards his mother's house. His mind was made up. He would woo and marry the goddess of Love. She was the only fitting bride . . .

Enkidu stepped out into his path.

Gilgamesh, deep in thoughts of marriage, moved to go round him. Enkidu stuck out a foot and tripped him up. Gilgamesh grabbed Enkidu's arm as he fell, and pulled him down, too. He was instantly enraged.

17

They wrestled in the doorways of the houses, their bulk smashing the door posts and bringing down the lintels. They grappled each other head-to-head, chest-to-chest, barging through the walls of buildings. First Gilgamesh was on his back, his face full of the Wild Man's hair, his nose bleeding, then the King was on top of Enkidu, their hands locked together. Scattering chickens, demolishing goat pens, overturning pails, the two men wrestled for fully an hour. Then Gilgamesh caught Enkidu off-balance, and with a twist of the body, hurled him to the ground.

Enkidu lay winded. Gilgamesh, hands clasped on knees, snorted out a triumphant laugh as he struggled to catch his breath. Then Enkidu too laughed. Lying on his back, he saw the fearful stars blinking down between the high buildings and laughed out loud. "There's not another man in the world like you, Gilgamesh!"

Gilgamesh sat down with his back against a wall. It was an unfamiliar feeling—to be tired out. The two men looked at one another. Then Enkidu flexed his arms and Gilgamesh flexed his, and they fell on each other again.

But this time it was an embrace. They hugged each other with the passion of new friends who know that they will stick together through thick and thin, come what may, do or die.

3 Do or Die

Like the axe in his dream, Gilgamesh wore Enkidu at his side and swore never to be parted from him. "I must have been mad to contemplate marriage," he told Enkidu, "especially to Ishtar!"

Gilgamesh schooled Enkidu in the ways of civilization, and then Enkidu taught him the way of the wild places: how the honey-ant gathers its winter food, how mistletoe grows without a root, how water can be mined out of the driest desert.

They wrestled and raced and hunted and talked, and the people of Uruk breathed a sigh of relief and gave thanks to the gods.

Enkidu had roamed far afield, into the wildest places. He had seen things which Gilgamesh had never seen. He had swum in both the Tigris and the Euphrates, had stood on the summit of Mount

Nisir where the ark ran aground after the Great Flood; had seen the monstrous Huwawa, Protector of the Cedar Forests, and the Scorpionmen who guard the roadway to the Garden of the Gods. One day, as Gilgamesh showed Enkidu the sights of the city, he pointed out the carved stone friezes recording the deeds of Uruk's great men.

"Where are the deeds of Gilgamesh?" asked Enkidu.

"Here!" cried Gilgamesh spread-eagling himself against the wall. "This blank. So far I've done nothing worth carving in stone. But soon! Soon, Enkidu! You and I are going on such an adventure that no wall will be large enough to record it!"

"We are?" Enkidu too flattened himself against the wall, striking a grand pose. "Where? When? Now?" The very ends of his long hair crackled with energy.

"It was you who gave me the idea. Who's the most frightening foe in the whole world?"

Enkidu racked his brains. "Gilgamesh is. Ask his enemies."

Gilgamesh laughed. "Someone far more dangerous! We are going to fight Huwawa, Guardian of the Cedar Forests, and kill him and bring home cedarwood to build new gates for Uruk!"

Enkidu stepped away from the wall. "Ah, now, listen. You're forgetting, I've *seen* Huwawa. He's a monster among monsters! The trees are small alongside him. His strength is the stuff of legends. He never sleeps. When a fox stamps its paw sixty leagues away, Huwawa hears it. He lives for battle! He was made for no other purpose than to guard the forest. No one goes there, for fear of him . . . Besides, a kind of magic surrounds him. You can't go close without your strength ebbing away. If you had seen Huwawa . . ."

"I would have killed him already!" declared Gilgamesh. "We have to make our mark! Don't we? What are you afraid of?"

"Of getting killed," said Enkidu candidly.

Gilgamesh spread his arms high above his head as if reaching up to clutch the hems of the gods. "Then we'll have died gloriously, won't we? And our names will be written in clouds of glory on the noonday sky! . . . Fame is everything, Enkidu, isn't it? Why live if not to make a mark on the world? To blaze a trail through it! To do deeds worthy of remembrance! Do or die!" Both his fists were clenched, his feet set square on to life, like a prize-fighter.

A surge of love and pride thrilled through Enkidu. "Do or die!" he cried, and closed his own hand around the King's upraised fist. "Just do me one favor. The Cedar Forest belongs to Shamash the Sun. Don't fly in the face of the gods. Tell Shamash what you want to do. Ask his blessing."

That is how Gilgamesh came to be standing, at high noon, in the full glare of the sun, a white kid at his feet, and in his right hand a silver scepter which caught the sunbeams as he spoke. "O Sun! O lord and master, who sees all! Only help me do this thing, and I shall build you a temple all of cedar wood—wood from your own forests. O Sun, you who are robed in fiery splendor, surely you understand a man's need to cloak himself in glory?"

Swaying as he prayed, Gilgamesh felt the tears on his cheeks dry to streaks of white salt. Then it was as if a red hot hand rested on the crown of his head. Shamash had given his blessing.

Crowds of curious onlookers had gathered, round-eyed, fearful, wondering. "*People of Uruk!*" cried Gilgamesh. "I go to the Forest of Cedar Trees, to cut cedar for new city gates and a temple to the god Shamash! There I shall do battle with Huwawa, the Evil One. Pray for me, and make offerings to the Sun. I shall bring back such glory to Uruk that the name of Uruk will live forever in the annals of the world!"

The crowd gave a nervous laugh and burst out singing. A clumsy, shuffling dance carried them home to their houses.

Gilgamesh and Enkidu went to the forges and gave orders for two axes and two swords. Armorers and craftsmen went out into the ancient groves and cut willow and box wood for axe handles and spear shafts. But they sent to Anshan in Persia for wood fine enough to make the King's bow. The axe of Gilgamesh was called "Might of Heroes," his bow "Anshan." Every stage of the craftsmanship was watched over by Gilgamesh and Enkidu, for they knew that their lives would depend on these weapons.

As the golden sparks flew up from the anvil, the elderly counselors of Uruk gathered in the doorway of the forge. Their old heads were white with the snow of wisdom. "You are young, Gilgamesh. Youth is rash. We beg you to reconsider. This Huwawa is a thing of spirit and magic—invincible!"

But Gilgamesh only laughed. "What do you want me to do, gentlemen? Sit at home for three score years? Wrap up warm in winter and keep cool in the summer, and stay safe here in Uruk?" The blacksmith passed a finished sword into his outstretched hands. It weighed as much as a grown man, but he handled it as delicately as a new-born baby.

23

The counselors shook their wise old heads. There is no telling young people anything they do not want to hear. They comforted themselves on the way home, saying, "If anyone can do this thing, it is Gilgamesh and his friend, the Wild Man."

Ninsun, the King's mother, sent for Enkidu. "Remember to dig a well every evening, Enkidu, and offer up pure water to the Sun God every day . . . Oh, look after him, Enkidu! You are not my son: I did not give birth to you. But bring Gilgamesh safe home and I shall adopt you as my own. I'm relying on you, Enkidu!"

The Wild Man bowed his head. For the first time, he realized that there was someone else in the world who loved Gilgamesh as much as he did.

What a way it was to the land of the cedar forests! Even though the friends walked fifty leagues a day, and accomplished in three days what it would take others six weeks to do, they still had seven mountains to cross before they stood at the forest gate.

Carved in a dozen languages were warnings and prohibitions:

"DO NOT ENTER"

"CUT NO TREES, ON PAIN OF DEATH"

"THIS FOREST IS PROTECTED BY HUWAWA, TERROR OF THE EARTH"

And yet the woodlands beyond the gate were as greenly peaceful as the bottom of a lake. Birdsong rippled outwards from it in tinkling wavelets. Enkidu shoved open the gate.

His knees sagged. His head spun. His hands prickled as

though stabbed by a thousand splinters. He jumped awkwardly backwards. "Gilgamesh! Don't go in there! The magic is too strong! The moment I touched the gate, my strength failed me!"

But Gilgamesh was already whistling his way along the broad green pathways of the wood.

In the center of the forest stood a green mountain—a perfect cone rising up so high that its peak was hidden by cloud. Its peaceful slopes seemed a perfect place to sleep. Without even troubling to dig a well and refill their water skins, the friends stretched out on the ground. Still, they slept hand-in-hand, so as to wake one another at the first sign of danger.

At midnight, Enkidu woke to the feeling of his knuckles being crushed together. Gilgamesh was sitting bolt upright, his eyes glistening in the dark. "I had a dream!" he said. "I dreamt the top of the mountain melted, and the earth spewed out its blood—fire and molten rock, and so much smoke and ash that the sun turned black. What does it mean?"

Enkidu laughed and extricated his hand. "It means we've come to the land of volcanoes, friend," he said. "In this part of the world the mountains erupt like spots on a young man's cheek. What else did you dream?"

"I dreamt that the earth trembled under me, and clouds of dust flew up so that I couldn't breathe, couldn't see, and

25

everything around me caught fire like kindling! What kind of portent is that for the gods to send me? What does it mean?"

Again Enkidu laughed. "It means we are in the land of earthquakes! Do you know nothing? The world's skin is like the skin of a lizard—now and then the scales twitch, and the earth shakes. What else did you dream?"

"I dreamt a bull," said Gilgamesh, his teeth chattering at the memory of it. "Not just a bull, I mean: a giant of a bull—bigger than twenty bulls. It was head-down and charging right at you, and there was nothing I could do! Nothing! Nothing!"

Enkidu scratched his head. "Huwawa is nothing like a bull," he said, puzzled. "His face is like a lion and he has fangs like a dragon. I don't know why you should dream a . . . Gilgamesh?"

But Gilgamesh had fallen asleep, his head on Enkidu's shoulder. When daylight came, he was still sound asleep. Enkidu touched him. Enkidu shook him. Enkidu took hold of him by the ears and banged his head on the ground, but he would not wake up. He was under the influence of Huwawa's magic.

The whole day came and went, and still Gilgamesh slept. Enkidu was panic-stricken. "*Wake up!*" he bellowed in his friend's ear. "*Wake up!* Must I tell your mother that I let you die in your sleep? Do you want Huwawa to find you like this?"

He slapped Gilgamesh. He rolled him down the hill. He held their empty water skins over his friend—oh, why had he not heeded Ninsun's advice? Enkidu dug and dug, but found no water. He ran and ran, until pebbles flew from under his feet as sparks had from the blacksmith's hammer. At last he heard the soft tinkle of trickling water. Splashing into the stream, he scooped the water skin through the cool, delicious water. Then back he ran and, upending the bag, emptied it in the King's face.

At last, the dark brown eyes opened. Stretching himself, Gilgamesh picked up his breast plate and put it on. He was perfectly calm. "Let us go and meet our enemy."

Enkidu kicked aside his bow in disgust. "You go if you like, but I'm going back to the city. You have no idea . . . You don't know what you are up against! Me, I'll go back and tell your mother how brave you are, how heroic, how glorious . . . how dead."

Gilgamesh calmly strung his bow. "Don't launch the funeral barge yet. What can go wrong with the two of us side by side?"

"Do you really want me to tell you?" said Enkidu.

Inside his cedarwood house, the giant Huwawa cocked his giant head on one side and listened. A smile came to his lips which curled like the bark from a silver birch. He reached out and took down his first cloak of splendour. Six more hung alongside it, woven out of magic and the fibres of the forest. He opened his door, stuck out his head and bellowed.

"WHO HAS COME INTO THE FOREST? LET HIM DIE!"

All the acorns fell from the trees—all the nests of the previous spring. He looked, and as he looked, the beam of his looking scythed down trees. He nodded his head, and malign magic rolled through the forest, bluer and deeper than drifts of bluebells. Then he stepped out of doors. The green forest was like grass around his feet. He blotted out the sun.

Gilgamesh, caught in the coal-black shadow, looked up. "Oh, Enkidu," he said. He had never thought anything could be so big.

Then Shamash the Sun looked down and saw Gilgamesh and his friend like two tiny ants in the path of an elephant's stampede.

The Sun breathed in, fetching the warm winds. He reached out to sea and grasped the north wind and the waterspouts, lightning and phosphorescent fire. He turned about and about, and the elements were twisted into a single whiplash, its thongs sharp with hail and sleet.

But the Guardian only ran back into his house and grabbed his second cloak. He had been formed to protect the forests, and even the master of those forests could not call him to heel.

Gilgamesh was wielding his axe now, hacking at the outermost wall of the lodge to bring it down. Seven walls, one inside another, and inside the seventh the Guardian, bellowing flame and destruction. Huwawa put on the third of his seven cloaks.

But with every passing moment, more of the winds of Heaven piled up around the cedarwood lodge. They turned back Huwawa's powers like a mirror turns back light. The Guardian put on the fourth of his seven cloaks, and the walls of his lodge bowed outwards, so great was the magic within. Huwawa put on the fifth and sixth of his seven cloaks and for twenty thousand leagues, the cedar forests trembled.

At last the seventh cedar wall fell, and Gilgamesh and Enkidu, axes in hand, came face to face with Huwawa. Seven cloaks billowed round him like the rays of a rainbow; magic shone from his open mouth, from the heels of his hands, from the fabric of his skin. Huwawa might be terrible, but he was also magnificent.

Suddenly, a cyclone of twisted wind and heat bound him round: he was powerless to strike the heroes dead. "Let me go, Gilgamesh!" he said. "Spare me and I shall be your slave, and cut down the trees myself to build you a fitting palace."

Gilgamesh hesitated. He glanced sideways at Enkidu.

"Don't listen to him!" urged Enkidu. "It's a trick. Kill him!"

Gilgamesh swung back his axe over one shoulder. "But, Enkidu . . . if we kill him, all that glory will be lost to the world forever!"

"Don't let him fool you, Gilgamesh!" (He was not at all sure how long those ropes of wind binding Huwawa's arms would hold him, how long before the giant would squirm free.)

It took three blows to despatch the Guardian of the Forests. He sprawled on his face, the trees falling flat for acres around. The phosphorescent glory which had hung about Huwawa went out like a blown candle. He was a mound of vegetable matter, a hummock in the landscape.

Dead.

Gilgamesh, walking the length of the Guardian's dead body, felt the spark of life flare up inside his own. He had survived! He was alive—even more alive than before. All the colors of the forest were more bright, the birdsong sweeter, the smells more delectable. The touch of his friend's hand on his arm made him dizzy with joy.

They found the tallest cedar tree in the entire forest and hacked it down. It fell with a deafening hiss of leaves. From this the carpenters of Uruk would fashion a mighty gate to the city.

Then, in reverence to the Sun, Gilgamesh washed himself in the river, put on clean robes and made an offering of cold water to Shamash, holding up the silver bowl while the noonday heat drank it up in steamy white sips.

And looking down, Ishtar, goddess of Love, saw the finest sight the world had to offer—a young man, covered in glory, triumphant, silhouetted against the sinking sun, a silver bowl upraised, face shining with pent-up happiness—King Gilgamesh.

4 Marry Me

"Gilgamesh! Gilgamesh! How well you look in my Temple of Love!"
Gilgamesh spun round.

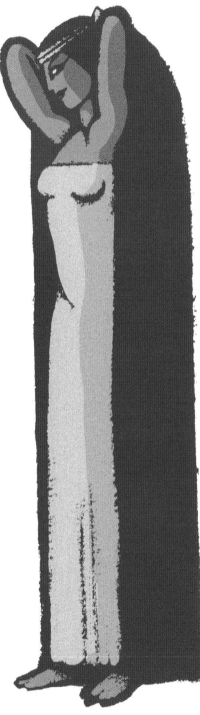

Through the perfumed smoke of the temple came a woman astounding in every way, swaying her hips, lifting her hair from the nape of her neck with both wrists. That hair! It spilled down like wine over-brimming a beaker, from the crown of her head to the soles of her feet. It was Ishtar, goddess of Love.

Enkidu's heart sank, for he could see that Ishtar was in love. She would twine her slender brown arms around Gilgamesh, and Enkidu's new-found friend would be lost to him. For who could resist the goddess of Love? He crept away into the daylight.

"Gilgamesh," said Ishtar, "killing Huwawa was a feat worthy of a god! My heart was in my mouth as you fought. Now it is in my hands. Think, Gilgamesh, if I were to give that heart to you. Think! I would make you a chariot of lapis with golden wheels. Kings and princes would lie like carpet under your feet. I could give you storm demons to pull your wagons. Nothing less will do for a husband of mine!"

She brought her face close up against his. Her breath smelt of nutmeg and roses. "I love you, King of Uruk. Marry me."

Gilgamesh breathed her in. The perfume made him dizzy. Then resting his hand on her upper arms, he said, "I'll pay you all the prayers and sacrifices a devout man ought to pay to a goddess. I always have and I always will. But as for marrying you . . . Oho!" He sucked the air in through his teeth. "Not for all the honey in the hive, lady." And he stood her away from him as if he were sliding a chair back under a table.

Ishtar's jaw dropped. A tendril of hair found its way into her mouth and she spat it out again, blinking, astounded.

"I'm flattered you should woo me," Gilgamesh went on, "but frankly I'd rather play dice with a handful of scorpions. I've heard about the men that you've loved in the past and I've heard what became of them once you lost interest. Being loved by you is rather like being struck by masonry falling off a high building, isn't it?"

Walking round and round her, he counted off on his fingers all the young men who had ever caught the eye of Ishtar.

"Remind me. What became of your husband—Tammuz? Such a devoted lover! When your sister was holding you prisoner in the Underworld, who took your place? Tammuz—the only person fool enough to spend eternity in the dark so that his true love could live in the sunlight.

"Take that shepherd—remember? The one who brought you

mealy cakes and roasted his fluffy little kids for your supper—played flute tunes to you on a bone whistle. He thought he was the happiest man alive—till you tired of him and turned him into a wolf. Where is he these days? Still carrying his tail between his legs? Still howling at the moon?

"And didn't you love the king of the Lions once? The one who died in those traps you dug for him. And that horse that took your fancy? Spurs and a whip, that was his reward in the end. You rode him seven leagues with spurs and a whip, then let him slake his thirst in muddy water.

"Take that bird who sang for you—the one with the multicolored plumes. When you tired of him, you smashed him like a ball with a racket, and now he sits on a branch and weeps, 'My wing! My wing! My poor broken wing!'"

Ishtar opened and shut her mouth, but no words came out.

"Oh, and that gardener, who tended your father's date palms? Does he enjoy being a mole, would you think? The trouble with you, madam, is that you start by kissing and end by cursing. I know you, lady, and I'd sooner wear tight shoes for the rest of my life than be married to you!"

And with a laugh which set all the candle flames quivering, Gilgamesh dodged her clawing fingernails, skipped out into the clean, white sunlight and ran to find Enkidu.

Ishtar gave a gasping roar. "Oh!" She beat her fists against the walls. "*Oh!*" She stamped and flung herself about in an ecstasy of rage. "*Oohhhwwah!*"

She ran all the way to Heaven and threw herself down at her father's feet, weeping bitterly. "It's Gilgamesh!" she sobbed. "Destroy him! Let me destroy him! He has insulted me!"

Anu fingered his beard. "How? What did he say?"

"He listed all my lovers and what I had done to them!"

Anu said, "And? Did he slander you? Was it untrue?"

"He called me a . . . a . . ."

Anu leaned forwards expectantly. "Yes? What did he call you?"

"Falling masonry! A pair of tight shoes! . . . Why are you laughing? Never mind what he called me, the wretch! The vile, beastly, wicked, blaspheming nobody! He must be destroyed! Give me the Bull of Heaven to destroy Gilgamesh and his famous City of Streets! He slaughtered Huwawa, and now he has slighted me!"

Anu's amusement turned to dismay at the news of Huwawa's death. Here was a serious affront to mighty Enlil who had created the Guardian of the Cedar Forests. "Gilgamesh should not have pitted himself against the gods in such a way!"

"Then loose the Bull of Heaven, and destroy him!" cried Ishtar.

"Do you know what you are asking, Ishtar? If I loose the Bull of Heaven, it will be seven years before Uruk recovers. Famine and drought! Destruction! Have you thought of the innocent people who may die?"

Ishtar wagged a dismissive hand. "Yes, yes. The granaries are full. The people won't suffer . . . But Gilgamesh must! I demand that Gilgamesh pay for what he said. *Well?*" Her tears splashed like hot lead on the pavements of Heaven.

Anu looked at his daughter. Anger made her ugly, as it makes all faces ugly. Her man's beard came bristling through the skin of her jaw; her teeth were bared, her eyes bloodshot with shouting.

It was plain there would be no peace until Ishtar got her way.

"Not the Bull of Heaven, daughter. Choose some lesser punishment."

"If you don't give me what I want," hissed Ishtar, her voice so menacing that even Anu shivered, "I shall go now and smash the bolts on the gates of the Underworld. I shall loose all the souls of the Dead . . ."

"*Ishtar!*"

"Up they will come, shrieking and gibbering out of the ground, jostling shoulders with the Living. No one will quite know whether the man beside him is a ghost—or if the bride behind the veil has been dead since the Flood. Wait until the Dead become hungry and begin to EAT!"

Anu shuddered in disgust. "Stop, Ishtar . . ."

"The Dead loosed from the Underworld to *eat the Living!*"

"*Ishtar, enough!*"

"Well?"

"I shall loose the Bull of Heaven, daughter . . . But it grieves me that a man should be punished simply for speaking the truth."

In the city of Uruk, red dust trickled from the sandstone buildings and all the dogs began to bark. Cockerels crowed in the middle of the night, and dates fell from the palm trees in fat, black splats. The City of Streets was feeling the approach of the Bull of Heaven.

Then everyone in Uruk was awake and running—yelling and pointing out over the plain. The goddess Ishtar was coming out of the dawn, leading the Bull of Heaven, and no one had seen such a sight in the history of the world.

From the parapets of the city wall, Gilgamesh and Enkidu watched. The Bull was as big as a herd of elephants within the one hide. Its great dew-lapped throat swept the ground and its horns spread like twin waterspouts catching the light; plated in lapis lazuli, their shining blue bow was as huge as the prow and stern of a ship. Ishtar led it to the far bank of the river.

"How women do hate to be spurned," said Enkidu softly. He could smell the sweat in his friend's palms—smell his own fear, come to that. Here was Destruction made flesh.

Then it stamped, and there was no more thinking.

The Bull stamped and the earth simply opened up. Acres of ground subsided into a bottomless crevasse, and with it a hundred young men.

Again the Bull pawed the ground, head down, the ugly hump of its back quaking. Within the city, the granaries fractured like stone eggs, spilling grain. Carved friezes crazed and fell in shards. Towers swayed and crumbled into dust, and a twin-forked, jagged chasm yawned in the ground, swallowing up two hundred warriors of Uruk. The River Euphrates cascaded down into darkness.

A single scream of terror hung in the air: it had the color of red dust, and settled on Gilgamesh like blood.

At the third stamp, the very walls of Uruk wavered like sheets of water. Enkidu was jarred off his feet and struck his head against the parapet. Pain paralyzed him. It seemed to sing through his skull and unstring his spine. Then he was on his feet again: "Quick! Before it can charge the city gate!"

Launching himself off the high wall, Enkidu landed between the very horns of the Bull, grasping them like the shafts of a cart. The foam from its nostrils burst into his face, blinding him.

Gilgamesh leapt down as well, sword drawn.

"Well, friend? Didn't we say we would make a name for ourselves?" called Enkidu. "Strike behind the horns if you can!"

Bucking stiff-legged, turning and turning on the spot, the Bull of Heaven lashed Enkidu with its thick, hairy cable of a tail and sent him sprawling along its back. But Gilgamesh was there to vault over the nose and take hold of the horns in Enkidu's place, to wrench them round until the beast was brought to a standstill. Enkidu meanwhile slithered over the Bull's rump, grabbing the tail as he went, pulling it like a bell rope, hanging on even when the dust from under its iron hooves enveloped him in gritty darkness. Digging in with his heels, he hauled on the tail—quick, wrenching tugs which took its attention away from the flimsy gate, away from Gilgamesh straddling its neck.

There was a flash of light, a hiss and a thud, and the blade of Gilgamesh's sword drove home right up to its hilt in the arch of the Bull's neck—just between the nape and the horns.

For long seconds, the Bull held still, the foam dripping from its nostrils into a sudsy pool between its feet. Then it staggered

38

sideways, crashed against the walls of Uruk, lurched the other way. It stumbled as far as the river before falling into what little water was left, turning it blood red.

Enkidu sat on the ground, holding his head, and Hatti the dancing girl ran towards him, asking was he hurt, could she help? Up on the wall—a wall crazed now with jagged cracks—Ishtar the goddess of Love let out a howl of pure hatred.

Tears burst through her tightly shut lids, making runnels in the red dust which had painted her the color of rage. "See how they have butchered the lovely Bull of Heaven! Weep, women, at what they have done!"

And the women did begin weeping—not for the carcass lying in the river's mud, perhaps, but for the three hundred young men swallowed up by the earth, for the empty river, for the spoiled beauty of the city.

Enkidu was disgusted. He twisted off the Bull's back leg and shied it at Ishtar, as he might at a cat yowling on a wall. "If I could get my hands on you, I'd show you butchery!"

Gilgamesh stood on the body of the Great Bull. "See the horns, plated in lapis? I shall fill them with oil and offer the oil to my guardian gods! Then I shall hang them on the wall of my palace to remind me how I slew the Bull of Heaven!"

And the men, happy to be alive, cheered and carried Gilgamesh and Enkidu shoulder-high into the battered city. Through streets strewn with rubble, past broken pillars and burning buildings they carried Gilgamesh. He felt his everlasting fame assured.

"*Who fought the Bull of Heaven?*" he shouted, and the clamoring little boys shouted back, "*Gilgamesh! Gilgamesh!*"

"*Who killed the Bull of Heaven?*" he called out to a group of dancing girls watching the mob tumble by. The girls eyed one another uncertainly, lids still red with weeping. Then Hatti, the friend of Enkidu, stepped out of the shade into the sunlight: "*Gilgamesh and Enkidu!*" she called, in her high, singing voice. After that the girls too were running alongside, whooping and chanting, "*Gil-ga-mesh! En-ki-du! Gil-ga-mesh! En-ki-du!*"

Only the mothers and old women stood in their doorways, shawls drawn tight under their chins, silent.

And high on her tower, Ishtar, alone and disregarded, chewed on her plait of hair and cursed Gilgamesh under her breath. "Death to Gilgamesh and Enkidu. A curse on their friendship and on their happiness! Justice on their mortal heads!"

Enkidu's head ached where it had slammed against the wall. Throughout the celebrations, he felt a little sick. That night he slept a sleep of utter exhaustion, and to the beating of the drums in his head, he dreamed a dream.

The gods were gathered in conference. Anu, the father of gods, was there; so too was Enlil, god of heroes; Ea, the maker of Mankind; Nurgal of the Underworld; Ninurta, god of war . . . A small patch of brightness, which pained Enkidu too much to look at, he took to be Shamash the Sun. The gods stood shoulder-to-shoulder in a ring, their heads close together.

"My daughter is right," Anu was saying. "Someone must pay."

"And yet they fought well. No warrior ever fought better," said Ninurta.

"I would take two, but I will settle for one," said Nurgal.

Shut out by the circle of backs, Enkidu found it hard to hear. Apparently some crime had been committed. Shamash was speaking now. "It was Gilgamesh who killed Huwawa."

"But it was Enkidu who cut down the tallest tree."

As in all the worst dreams, Enkidu tried to speak, tried to put his side of the argument. But his hands would not lift and there was no breath in his lungs. His shouts only emerged in whimpers.

Shamash was saying, "Were they not, in a way, honoring us by these heroic deeds?"

Enlil rounded on Shamash. "The Bull of Heaven has been killed. Law demands the death penalty. It is simply a matter of deciding who shall die: Gilgamesh or Enkidu, Gilgamesh or Enkidu, Gilgamesh or Enkidu, Gilgamesh or . . ."

He woke with the name of his friend on his lips.

"Gilgamesh or . . ." He was wet with sweat and shivering. He had to go and tell Gilgamesh—to warn him. Dreams were not just the rotting vegetation of the past, the leaves blown down from the day before. Dreams were omens. Dreams were messages. He slipped his legs off the bed and tried to stand up.

But the roaring inside his head was like the Bull of Heaven bellowing. He covered his eyes, but the light still seared through to his brain. Sweat crawled down his body like a swarm of beetles, and his guts ached.

"Gilgamesh!" he tried to call, but his own name emerged instead. "Enkidu! Enkidu must die!"

5 Death

Gilgamesh sponged his friend's face and put a cup of water to his lips. "Soon be well, 'kidu. Soon be well." Enkidu turned his face away. The pain inside his head was like an axe-blow. "The gods say not. The gods say I must die."

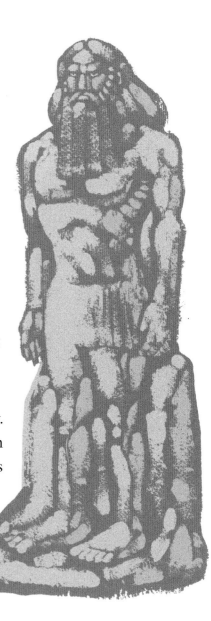

But Gilgamesh snorted dismissively. "Everyone dreams bad dreams when they're sick. Come on, man! Heroes like us aren't afraid of anything, are we?"

Two days later, Enkidu was powerless to sit up, unable to eat. A pulse of fear started up within Gilgamesh, despite himself. "Soon be well, friend," he kept saying, but Enkidu only groaned.

Something worse than misgiving seized on Gilgamesh. "I'll go to the temple, 'kidu. I'll go and pray for you. The gods will listen to me. Shamash listened before. I'll have the goldsmiths make a statue of you. Yes, I will! I'll tell them to make a golden statue of you and offer it up to the gods in place of the real thing! Why don't I do that? Yes! Wait here! Don't worry. You mustn't worry. Everything will be all right." And he was gone, running towards the temple, shouting commands, summoning his craftsmen.

Enkidu was left alone on his bed. The sun moved round, and a ray of sunlight like a fist punched through the window and struck him in the face. "Oh, Shamash, you faceless, orange clod, hear my curses!" he told the Sun. "Let my curse fall on that trapper who fetched me out of the Wild! Make him smell so bad that the beasts scent him twelve leagues off! Let him never catch another creature —not so much as a gerbil. Let him fall into his own pits. Let the lions tear him limb from limb!

"And Hatti! O, curse the dancing girl for me! Let all doors shut against her. Give her nowhere to sleep but the rubbish heap! I was happy before she came! Out there in the wilderness, I was happy. But she had to come along and daub me with kisses. She made the animals shun me—so let her be shunned!"

He broke off, panting for breath; his skull seemed to be squeezing the blood from his brain. The window-hanging blew out in a draft and set the sunlight dancing. The beams were full of motes, like stylus marks on a tablet of yellow clay, dancing too excitedly to be read. It seemed to Enkidu that a voice came rustling in at the window along with that breeze—a voice so soft and gentle that he had to strain to hear it.

"Enkidu. Oh, Enkidu. Why curse? Why curse the trapper? And why curse little Hatti? Without them, you would never have gone questing after Huwawa, never have fought the Bull of Heaven, never have written your name on history. The city would not now

43

be holding its breath, praying for Enkidu. Gilgamesh would not be kneeling now in the temple of the gods, weeping salt tears. Don't you see? Without Hunter and Hatti, you would never have met Gilgamesh! Now Gilgamesh will be the Wild Man. He will mourn you like a wolf baying at the moon and wander the world looking for comfort . . . Would you really choose to have lived without such a friend?"

Enkidu's fist closed around the empty air containing the sunbeam. "*I call them back! Every last curse! Be my witness, Shamash, I call them back!* Never have met Gilgamesh? Hunter, may your traps be full every morning! May your arrows never miss their mark! Never have met Gilgamesh? Hatti—little Hatti—let men twelve leagues away see you and swoon! Let kings stop their chariots to propose marriage. Let the gods lean out of Heaven to whistle at you! . . . Never have met Gilgamesh? That would have been never to have lived at all. We came alive together, he and I. We made sense of it all. We made sense . . ."

Enkidu let his hand fall. Fever made the room throb and crinkle like the walls of a bread oven, and his tears were scalding hot. And yet he was easier in his mind.

Gilgamesh came bounding back from the temple, hopeful, full of optimism. Now Enkidu would get better.

It took only one glance to know he was mistaken.

His friend's eyes were shut. Gilgamesh sank his fingers in his friend's hair and shook him. "Wake up! I thought you were . . ."

Then Gilgamesh cradled his friend in his arms and their tears soaked indistinguishable into the crumpled pillow.

For seven days Gilgamesh struggled, like a man swimming in

44

mid-ocean, trying to keep a friend afloat. Below them, in the depths, cruised Death. First it would swallow Enkidu and then, in the blinking of an eye, Gilgamesh. Life was nothing but treading water until the sharks came along . . .

"It's shameful for a man to die like this!" said Enkidu. "Ishtar hasn't just killed me; she has managed to shame me, too . . . Listen! Why is everywhere so quiet?"

Gilgamesh eased his arm from under Enkidu and stood up, stiffly. He went to the window with its broad sill, and stepped outside, high above the silent city. His voice carried loud over the early morning city. "Quiet? It's not quiet, friend! Can't you hear the people of Uruk weeping for Enkidu? Can't you hear them? The girls who brought you food, the bathhouse girls who rubbed oil into your back, the shepherds—all sobbing like children. Listen! And the friends you made—so many friends. And Hatti—little Hatti . . ." (He raised his voice still higher.) "You! You animals in the wilderness! You knew him in his wild days, and you're weeping for him, aren't you? You trees in the cedar forest—you're weeping for him, aren't you? Every place we ever went, every blade of grass we trod underfoot, every river we ever drank from—all the mountains and all the valleys—they're weeping for you! Everyone is mourning Enkidu. Listen! Can't you hear? *Why* can't you hear?"

He went back to the man on the bed, still shouting his lament. But Enkidu's eyes remained shut. Gilgamesh laid a hand on the Wild Man's heart, but knew he would feel no beat. "And me, 'kidu. And me. I'm weeping. *I'm* weeping for you, Enkidu. Wake up now. Wake up and see how the world prizes you. Don't sleep your life away. Wake up now. Don't get lost in the dark."

Gilgamesh covered his friend over with a sheet of silk, carefully, precisely, meticulously. Then he let loose the madness which he had kept at bay so long. He smashed everything precious, everything beautiful, ripping down hangings, hurling ornaments out of the window. He tore out his hair and pulled his clothes in shreds, twisting his knuckles white amid their rich fabrics.

Then, when the rage was past, he sat down again by his friend, panting, one hand on the silk. "Wake up now. Please wake up."

The whole household gathered outside the door, whispering anxiously, calling out, offering to carry the body away for burial. But Gilgamesh would not let them in. He fixed his eyes on his friend's shrouded face, and he willed the silk to stir. All that day he sat with the body. All of the next day, too.

He did not try to hold back his tears. For seven days and seven nights he watched them make their splashy patterns on the tiles at his feet. Then, on the eighth day he stopped crying.

46

Realization fell on him, like a ton of sand: no amount of crying was going to bring Enkidu back. His death went on forever.

He got up and opened the door. The smell of decay in the bedroom was choking.

Gilgamesh went outside into the sterile sunlight. The little golden statue of Enkidu, which he had commissioned as a bribe to the gods, stood on a table outside the Temple of Shamash. Beside it Gilgamesh set a red carnelian bowl filled with honey, and a bowl of lapis lazuli filled with butter—offerings to the gods.

After all, they were not really to blame, he mused, as flies droned in circles over the honey, and the butter changed from pale gold to a clear, translucent liquor. Mortal men are bound by the rules of Nature. From the moment of birth, they are heading towards their death. He would not curse Shamash or Anu or Enlil or Nurgal—or even Ishtar—for taking his friend away from him. It was unbearable, and yet it had to be borne. That was the paradox. Unbearable, and yet it had to be borne.

Just so long as they did not expect him, too, to die.

6 Afraid of Nothing

Gilgamesh meant never to die. Having seen death at close quarters, he knew that it was not for him. It made a nonsense of all endeavor, made fame worthless, made achievements hollow. No, he would oversee Enkidu's funeral, then leave Uruk—it held nothing for him now—and go in search of the secret.

"What secret? What is it you want to know?" his mother asked, alarmed by the unkempt wildness of her son and the look in his eye of sheer madness.

"The secret of immortality, of course," said Gilgamesh. "What I have to do, where I have to go to live forever."

"Oh, but Gilgamesh! Son!" Ninsun sat down, her hands in her lap. "No one lives forever! Death comes to us all in the end. It is just a matter of how . . ."

"*That's not true!*"

Ninsun was alarmed. Her son's voice was so strident. He grabbed her by the wrist and dragged her through the palace yards and gardens to where a frieze decorated one of the great walls.

As a child, Gilgamesh had sat and gazed at it for hours. It was his favorite story: of the Flood and the man who saved the world from ending. The boat riding on the floodwaters was just a square —a simple box—and on top of it stood a man, hands upraised. "*He* didn't die!" Gilgamesh jabbed a finger at the sailor on the frieze. "Utnapishtim was granted immortality by the gods. If they can grant it to him, they can grant it to me! All I have to do is find Utnapishtim and ask him the secret!"

Ninsun trembled for her son. The death of his friend had driven him to desperation. He was not eating, not washing, not sleeping. Already his handsome face had aged ten years. She put out a hand to touch his cheek, but she might as well have reached out for a bird. He broke away from her and was gone—a wild, disheveled creature running away. "Gilgamesh! Son! Come back! Where are you going? *Come back!*"

The King of Uruk ran out into the wilderness. Soon his hair, once so curled and glossy, hung in a dusty, matted mass down his back, past his waist, and his kingly robes were ragged. He drank at the same muddy waterholes as gazelles and hogs.

He asked the beasts and the bushes and the trees, "Where can I find Utnapishtim?" but they did not answer. The trees only put their heads together and whispered. He despised them. They lived and died without a struggle. He envied them: each spring they came back to life. Not Enkidu. He would never come back.

He did not stop to eat. In the stony wilderness, there was precious little food to be had anyway, and he was always thirsty.

49

The fat melted off him like sacrificial butter, leaving his shanks thin, his wrists and ankle-bones looking over-large. In the daytime the sun burned him raw, and sweat trickled down his hair in droplets. By night, the cold was so terrible that blood from a cut froze before it touched the ground. But on he went, as if Death were dogging his trail. At last he came within sight of the Mountains of Mashu— an awesome sight to a man of the plains.

So high that they pierced the sky itself, so jagged that they sawed land from sky, they recalled memories of his earliest childhood. As a boy, his father had brought him this far on a hunting expedition. The memory even now made the hairs stand up on the nape of his neck. Lions. He remembered lions—such numbers of lions that the journey had been abandoned.

"O moon god Sin!" he prayed aloud, as a full moon bobbed up like a bubble from behind the mountains. "Guard my sleeping hours and bring me safely through this night."

He walked into the foothills until daylight failed completely, then he climbed into a tree and slept. When he woke, it was a moment before he remembered where he was. His eyelids were gummy with dust from the plains. He rolled over and only narrowly saved himself from falling out of the tree. Beneath him, dancing and prancing, playfully wrestling and rolling on their backs in the dew were thirty or forty lions, lionesses, cubs. Their golden bodies were lithe as river water. They glowed with health and energy, absolute rulers of their sunny habitat.

And Gilgamesh hated them for being so alive.

He leapt out of the tree, sword drawn, teeth clenched. He caught them by their tails and smashed them one against another, jumped and stamped on them, wrestled and throttled them, maddened by the joy they took in life. Afterwards he ate lion steak and replaced his city clothes with a lion's pelt knotted by the paws around his neck. Now the big, lifeless paws patted against his skin as he walked. It soothed him, that the lively lions were dead.

Beyond the foothills, the Mashu mountains rose up, sheer, and smooth as glass, a barricade between the lands of men and the Garden of the Gods. There was a gate, a way through. The sun itself, in sinking at night, used the gate to pass through the mountain. But Gilgamesh had not reckoned with the monsters who stood guard over the gate, the Scorpionman and Scorpionwoman.

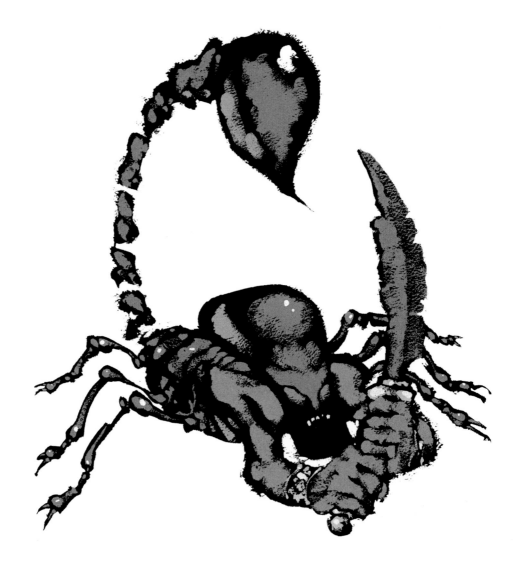

Their heads were helmeted with smooth black scales, the eyes lost somewhere behind their flaring nostrils, the beards (both man and woman) as black as thunderclouds. Their lower bodies—balanced on crackling, scuttling legs, were invulnerable to arrows or fire or sandstorm—to the heat of the sun as it rolled past them each evening, to the cold of the darkness which followed. And arching over each head, like a great bulbous black mace, hung the poisonous tip of a scorpion's tail.

They rarely had cause to use their stings. The very sight of them sucked a man's heart flat, drained it of blood, left him whitely dead

52

of shock. When they saw Gilgamesh striding out towards them, they were both astonished and intrigued.

"He must be one of the immortals," said Scorpionman.

"Two parts, yes," said Scorpionwoman, "but one part is human. Can you not smell it? Can you not smell flesh and blood?" She called out to Gilgamesh, "*Halt! Who dares approach?*"

"I am looking for Utnapishtim whom they call 'the Faraway' and who lives at the place called Paradise Shore, beyond the Garden of the Gods! My name is Gilgamesh, King of Uruk, and I believe this is the way I have to go!"

The Scorpion Beings trembled: a sound like a million land-crabs sloughing their shells. "To do that, you would need to travel through the mountain—twelve leagues without light! What is so important that you should attempt the impossible?" (They noticed that Gilgamesh's feet were never still; even now he trod water like a drowning man.)

"Open the gate and let me through. There are things I have to ask Utnapishtim—things no one else can tell me."

The Scorpion Beings marveled at his perseverance. "Are you not *afraid*, Gilgamesh? Do you know nothing of the fear that keeps your fellow men at home. We admire your courage, King of Uruk. We do! But turn back now, if you love life."

The expression then on Gilgamesh's face made even the Scorpion Beings blanch. His soul looked out at them through his eyes, and his soul was in torment.

"I had a friend," he told them, "the best friend a man ever had. His name was Enkidu. We did everything together. But my friend died. He *died*, you hear? I thought that if I argued for him, I could save him. I thought that if I held him in my arms, the gods couldn't take him away. I thought that if I cried long enough, my tears would bring him back to life. But I was wrong! Enkidu is dead and gone, and thanks to him—'Not afraid,' did you say? I'm so afraid I don't care if Scorpionmen stand in my way: it's all I can do to see the path in front of me—I'm so *afraid*! This 'Death' has turned me into such a coward that I can't sink any lower into fear. And what good is a king who's too afraid to sit in his own city? *What good is a hero eaten up with terror?*"

The Scorpion Beings laid aside their weapons. They heaved open the fire-scorched gate (which had only ever opened for the Sun). "Pass through before nightfall, Gilgamesh of Uruk. If you do not lose your wits in the dark, you may at last reach the Garden of the Gods. And may the gods grant you an answer to your questions or an easy death."

For a while, when he looked back, Gilgamesh could see

their heads silhouetted against the tunnel's entry, dark against the daylight, watching him go. But then the tunnel's entrance was out of sight and he was plunged into unrelieved darkness.

Dark.

It was not the dark of night, pricked through with stars. It was not the darkness of indoors, with candles or embers in the grate. It was not the darkness of sleep which is illuminated by moonlight, or by dreams, at least. No, this was solid dark. The air was every bit as black as the rock walls to either side: no means of seeing his way forward, no way of knowing where the passage bent or its floor was aswarm with cockroaches. On and on Gilgamesh went, his fingers touching the wall to either side, his face pushing forwards, his eyeballs dry with staring helplessly after light. The darkness had struck him blind and he had to feel his way, step by chilling step. When he looked back after one league—dark. When he looked forwards—dark. Inside and outside of his eyelids—dark. Filling his brain—dark.

After two leagues there was no difference, no shaft of light, no movement of air. Dark to front and back. Dark inside and out. Dark.

After four and after five leagues, the darkness seemed to seep through his skin. He could taste, smell, see, and hear only darkness. The mountain was digesting him.

After six leagues, after seven, there was still no relief. He knew what it was to be cut off from Shamash, out of touch with his god, buried alive under fathomless rock. It was almost like being dead.

After eight, after nine leagues he might as well have been born without eyes. He thought that if he were not already mad with grief, then this darkness would have done for him.

After ten leagues a breeze flowed into his face like black water. After eleven, he thought his mind must be playing tricks on him, for a pinprick of light seemed to be dancing, far away, small as an ant's egg. As he felt his way forward, the pinprick grew to a circle, and through the circle strayed a few weak rays of light.

Blinking and stumbling and blinkering his eyes with both hands, he ran out of the tunnel and into . . .

. . . a garden.

It was a garden like no other, for instead of fruit or blossoms on the trees, jewels and precious stones bent the golden branches under their glittering weight: carnelian and agate, emeralds and peridots, zircons and opals. Jet pips encased in ruby berries, lapis leaves flickering, pearls as big as snowberries, branches of coral on trees of onyx, all tinkled and twinkled amid umbelliferous flowerheads of silver. Even the dew was diamantine.

After the dark, the absurd magnificence dazzled Gilgamesh. He smiled, despite himself, but found the muscles of his face wasted; he could only smile deadpan.

Well, he thought despite his weariness. I have come this far. If I can do that, I can do more. Then the words of his friend came back to him like stones to choke on:

"Do or die!"

No truer words.

Do or die.

7 Give Up

Beyond the garden was the even greater brightness of the sea.
Gilgamesh stood toe-to-toe with the surf, and stared out across the
water, perplexed. The sea? He had heard of it but never seen it.
He looked around for help.

Then he saw it—a sea-front bar, its terrace overhung with vines. There was a wine-press, too. Whoever lived here clearly grew the grapes, pressed them and fermented the wine before selling it to passers-by. What passers-by? A woman as big as an oak cask sat skimming the scum off a vat of newly pressed juice. A veil concealed all but her big bare feet.

Gilgamesh could not see her face through the veil, but she could see him. As he came into view, she straightened a little, then throwing down her skimmer and hoisting up her skirts, she ran for the safety of the house. He saw what she was doing and put on a sprint, but she was already inside and slamming the door. He put out one foot and wedged it in the closing gap.

Siduri leaned the whole of her bulk behind the door. Gilgamesh yelped and withdrew his foot. The woman managed to pin the door shut with her great weight. "*Go away, whoever you are!*"

Gilgamesh put his mouth close to the door and bellowed, "Let me in or I'll smash in your walls and kick your wine-press into the sea! I am Gilgamesh, King of Uruk, slayer of Huwawa and the Bull of Heaven!"

"No you're not!"

"Yes, I am!"

"Not!"

"Am!"

"Not!"

"I've heard of Gilgamesh," she panted back through the door, "and he's young and handsome and all the women of Uruk swoon after him with his big dark eyes and his curly hair! And you come along telling me you're Gilgamesh, you . . . you . . . you old *candlewick*!"

Gilgamesh was taken aback. He stepped away from the door, and Siduri, who had been pushing on it with all her weight, spilled out of doors at his feet. But she was unrepentant. "Look at you!" she said. "You look 104, and as if you've seen all the trouble of the world! Look as if you've walked half the world and slept out in all weathers without so much as a hat! All skin and bone and worry, that's you," she said accusingly. "Call yourself Gilgamesh of Uruk?"

"I am!"

"Not!"

"Am!"

"Not!"

"Am!"

"Look at yourself!"

So Gilgamesh did look into a bowl of skimmed grape juice, and even he doubted that the reflection looking back at him was

Gilgamesh of Uruk. His cheeks were hollow, his eyes sunken into their sockets, his lips blistered by heat and chapped by cold. His beard was matted with filth, and his hair had turned snow white. He slapped the reflection into fragments. "Why shouldn't I be changed?" he said. "I've traveled half the world, and I have had troubles. You wouldn't understand—how could a woman understand. I had a friend. The best friend a man could have. His name was Enkidu, and I loved him. Now he's dead. I've just walked through twelve leagues of darkness, and unless I can find Utnapishtim the Faraway—I shall die just like Enkidu. Isn't that grief enough to change a man?"

During the wild and furious lament, Siduri had got to her feet and busied about righting tables and polishing a cup on her veil. "Sit down and have a drink," she said cozily. "A few raisins, look. Some good fresh bread: I baked it this morning." She hummed tunelessly and threw a rock at a seagull stealing sardines from the drying rack. Gradually Gilgamesh grew calmer and dried his tears with one paw of his lion skin.

"Tell me how I can find Utnapishtim, woman," he said.

"Get washed first, and have a bite to eat . . . It can't be had, you know."

"What can't?"

"This immortality thing." She went and filled a beaker with seawater to throw at the skinny cats basking on her roof. "When the gods made us, they never meant us to last. No more than a loaf of bread or a chicken's egg. We was meant to grow up, grow old, and fall off the twig. You know what you ought to do?"

59

"Find the Paradise Shore, not sit here wasting time . . ."

"Give up, my dear! Eat, drink, and be merry—did you never hear that? Eat, drink, and be merry . . . Oooh, I can recommend it! Honeycakes for breakfast, freshly grilled sardines for lunch, milk and pobs after a supper of eggs. Melon! Now what did the gods ever invent that was better than a melon, eh? Except two melons. A lobster—oooh. Who needs paradise? You're a long time dead—there's another true thing for you. You're a long time dead. Grab the day and run with it. What you ought to do is *get married*. Children. That's the shape of happiness. A little hand inside yours. Someone riding high up on your shoulders, laughing out loud. Friends, yes. But a good wife takes some bettering. Cherries in bed. Someone to sit with in the shade. Someone who can weather you even when you're sour as a lemon. Someone who thinks all your jokes are funny. Someone who knows what you like to eat after a hard day's . . . whatever it is a king does. Someone who thinks you're as much a hero for killing a cockroach as a dragon. Get married and have children! That's the way we foil the gods. I mean what good would it do you to live a million years unhappy?"

The cats came coiling and moiling back to their favorite spot.

"Keep your advice for your customers. Just tell me where I can find Utnapishtim."

Siduri sucked in air through her teeth, so that her veil puckered against her mouth. "Oho, now he lives over the water—t'other side of the Waters of Death. And no one crosses over there but Urshanabi the ferryman. He fetches and carries things over to Paradise Shore. You could always ask him . . . but he won't take you anyway. Against his terms of employment, see? Be better off giving up and going home. Seems to me, it's the quality of life that matters, not how long it drags on . . . *Shoo!*"

Siduri lunged at the cats, flapping her skirts, sending them yowling and hissing down the beach. When she turned, Gilgamesh had gone. Siduri chose herself the fattest sardine, poured herself a cup of wine, and with her feet resting in the water-bucket, ate lunch, flinging the fishheads and tails to the cats and the seagull, as they had known very well she would; she did it every day.

Ocean. The edge of all geography, the margin of the Known World. Out there, what monsters lurked under the brittle glass roof of moving water? Gilgamesh's fright fueled a spitting ungovernable anger even he did not understand.

Suddenly he saw it, bobbing on turquoise shallows amid the pincushion pines—the ferry to Paradise Shore. The ferryman was applying a coat of paint to the snake-headed prow.

Well, thought Gilgamesh, if it had to be done, he would do it as he had always done things—with heroic violence. He would capture this boat, as he had captured the cities of the plains! So opening his mouth and emptying his mind, Gilgamesh ran down out of the trees, hollering and yelling and dragging his sword point through the noisy pebbles. He hurtled up to his knees in the water and began smashing at the boat's stern.

Over and over again he hacked at the pegs and pulley and cleats and magic symbols. Out of the corner of his eye, he was aware of the ferryman gaping at him.

61

Missing his footing, Gilgamesh slipped on a weed-covered stone and sat down with a splash. The ferryman threw his paintbrush in the air. "Now what did you want to go and do that for?"

"*You have to take me over to Paradise Shore!*" Gilgamesh demanded. "*You have to take me to Utnapishtim the Faraway!*"

Urshanabi covered his eyes with one hand. "You've made good and sure I don't, haven't you? You just smashed the steering gear and the magic that drives her where the wind won't."

Gilgamesh felt suddenly rather small. He pulled himself to his feet and declared that being a king gave him the right to smash boats as and when he saw fit. "I am Gilgamesh of Uruk, Slayer of Huwawa and the Bull of Heaven!"

"Then you must have fallen on hard times," said the ferryman. "I heard you were young and too full of life for your own good. And here you are, looking like the bones left on a gutting table after the catch is landed. What happened to you?"

So Gilgamesh told him: "I had a friend. His name was Enkidu. When the gods decreed he must die, I was made to look Death in the face, and the sight terrified me. Terrified. I can't die like that. I can't die. Utnapishtim didn't! So he can tell me the secret of immortality." Little by little, the slopping sea washed all the bluster and aggression out of Gilgamesh, and he was left explaining himself, excusing himself. "Don't be angry with me, ferryman. You go there every day. All I'm asking is that you take me there once."

Urshanabi shook his big, sunburned head and skipped a stone over the waves. "You ask more than you know . . . But since the steering gear is smashed . . . I'll need you to cut twelve good long poles of wood from the tallest trees you can find. Then whittle and ream them so that they slot together, end to end. Can you do that?

Can kings turn their hands to such work? Thing is, man of Uruk, the crossing takes us over the River of Death. If you or I so much as dip one finger into that water—or splash ourselves with its spray —we'll discover all the secrets of *mortality* then and there, quicker than was meant."

Humbled, Gilgamesh did as he was told, though he could not tell why exactly they should need twelve poles of wood.

He discovered soon enough. Putting out to sea along the pathways left by the sinking sun, thinking every moment to tumble over the edge of the world, Gilgamesh was obliged to punt. One pole was long enough for a while, to touch bottom, but soon two screwed together end to end were not long enough. He screwed on a third and a fourth, feeling the tip far below skid and skip over —what?—the hulls of sunken ships? The shells of sleeping turtles? The skulls of drowned men? The scales of sea monsters? Soon six rods were not long enough.

Some time during the night they crossed into a sea lane which thrummed and raced under the hull, making the boat roll and yaw till Gilgamesh was as green as a snake. "Don't let your hands touch the water!" warned Urshanabi, and Gilgamesh knew that they were crossing the River of Death. Not seven nor eight rods, not nine or ten were enough to touch the bottom of this deepest ocean trench. Gilgamesh screwed on the eleventh and then the very last rod he had cut from the seaside forest.

But Urshanabi had miscalculated.

"It's not enough!" he told the ferryman. The fast sea current was starting to carry the boat off course. What would happen if he was forced to push his hand and wrists into the waves in order to touch bottom? Would the oily darkness seize on him like tar, or wash the life out of him through the palms of his blistered hands?

Then he thought of the mast.

"But without a sail how shall we break free of the current?" Urshanabi protested, as Gilgamesh hacked down the mast.

"*I* shall be the mast!" said Gilgamesh.

Using the mast for a thirteenth rod, their punt pole was at last long enough to touch bottom, and Gilgamesh was able to punt on across the River of Death, his hands staying clear of the water. Then Urshanabi took the punt pole, and Gilgamesh put on Urshanabi's shirt—his body was so wasted and thin that it flapped round him like a shroud. He stood amidships, arms stretched out to either side, and the west wind filled the shirt, which bellied out ahead of him.

He thought he must be carried away by the wind, blown into the sky among the wheeling seagulls.

"It can't be done, you know," Urshanabi called over his shoulder, casual, matter-of-fact. "The gods never meant people to live forever. Not your friend, not you, not me. You can ask Utnapishtim, but he'll tell you the same. You should stop fretting about death and settle for a good life—do things you can look back on with pride. Make your mark on the world, by all means! But then pass the baton to the next runner. That's the way of the world. Run with the baton, then pass it on!"

The boat slowed. Urshanabi turned and saw that Gilgamesh was no longer holding his arms at full stretch, but had his fingers in his ears, so as not to hear the ferryman's talk of giving up.

8 Faraway

What would he be like, Utnapishtim
whom the gods had rewarded with eternal life?
Would he look like Enkidu—thickset and shaggy?
Would he stand larger than life, skin radiating life like the zest
from a lemon?

As Gilgamesh stood, arms outstretched, catching the wind in Urshanabi's shirt, he saw the shore coming closer, and on it all manner of wonderful sights—a lion sleeping while a fawn calmly cropped grass within the circle of its paws; a wolf playing alongside a lamb. The air was full of the sound of wood pigeons crooning, and doves sat in heart-shaped pairs on leafy trees.

"No snow ever falls here," said Urshanabi the ferryman. "The animals live in perfect peace. There's no death for ravens to gloat over." On Paradise Shore only the hours and the years died imperceptibly, molting like feathers from a swan's back.

Then Gilgamesh caught sight of a middle-aged couple sitting together under a halub tree, he in a hammock cracking nuts, she busy brushing a little white goat.

At the approach of the boat, the man in the hammock shielded his eyes to look. He had large, sticking-out ears, a thin neck and protruding teeth.

"There he is, man of Uruk," said the ferryman. "Not that he will tell you anything different from what I've said."

Gilgamesh could hardly believe his ears. "*This* is Utnapishtim the Immortal? The Faraway?" Leaping ashore, he went and stood openly staring at the old man in the hammock.

He must have looked very menacing, but the man in the hammock did not stir. He simply asked, "Who are you?"

"I am Gilgamesh, King of Uruk!" he declared, bracing his shoulders, jutting his chin.

"My word," said the man, looking less than impressed, "the burdens of kingship must be great these days. Why so haggard and ragged—as if you had seen all the sufferings of the world?"

"Because I have!" said Gilgamesh. "I've crossed the desert, scorched by the sun and flayed by frost; traveled through twelve leagues of utter darkness; punted my way across the River of Death. And I have grieved, too. My friend Enkidu died and I've sworn never to suffer the same fate. That's why I've come—to learn the secret of immortality, from the one man who has it . . . I thought you would be more . . . more . . ."

"More what?" Utnapishtim smiled, amused by Gilgamesh's bewilderment. "More full of life? Raging and racketing about? Wrestling wild beasts to their knees? Slaying giants?"

"Yes! Yes, yes! Yes!" Without realizing it, Gilgamesh sat down on the ground, the fatigue of his journey suddenly overwhelming him. Utnapishtim's wife brought him a drink of wine.

"Why? Where's the hurry? What do I have to prove? When a man has only a few years of life, he feels he must pack them full. Say you were given a small trunk and told, 'You can carry away with you only as much as you can fit in here.' Then, naturally, you would cram it full, wouldn't you? Me, I have all the time in the world. Time is not standing at my back with his whip making me dance, making me run, making me strive. I've had time to learn the important things are few. A wife, contentment, memories, peace. You should not have put yourself to the trouble of coming all this way," he said at length. "It is your fate to live and then to die—just as it was mine to live forever."

"Ah, but I slew Huwawa!" boasted Gilgamesh. "And the Bull of Heaven! On my way here I slew a whole pride of lions!"

Utnapishtim nodded, less impressed than Gilgamesh would have hoped. "Might I venture to suggest," he said, "that the gods prefer their works of creation alive rather than dead?"

"Tell me," said Gilgamesh tersely. "Tell me how you came to be immortal." And while he listened he was thinking, at the back of his mind, What can this man do that I can't?

When Enlil began creating the world (said Utnapishtim) his workmen were his fellow gods—Anu and Ea and We-e and Nurgal. But long before the last river bed was dug, the gods threw down their spades and pickaxes and refused to do another stroke. Then We-e came up with a solution. They ought to create some kind of creature to complete the work. Thus human beings were created. They were ideal! When they could not work any more, they died. But there were still enough, because they reproduced themselves at

69

such a rate! Soon cities grew up, swarming like ant hills with industrious little people.

The only snag was the noise they made. All day long they quarreled and laughed, bartered goods in the markets, sang or made speeches. They left their babies out in the sunshine and the mewling and shrieking was more than Enlil could stand.

"*What is that noise?*" demanded Enlil.

"It's the people," said Ea. "Busy little things, aren't they?"

"*Thin them out!*" hissed Enlil, nerves frayed from lack of sleep. "Send Plague to prune the noisiest."

Ea did as he was told. But he had grown fond of humankind, and hurried off ahead of Plague, to warn them. When Plague arrived, the cities of Earth were silent as mirages, the citizens moving about their business wordlessly, the market traders miming, the babies' mouths plugged up with honeycomb.

And while they remained silent, Enlil was content to let them live. But as time passed, of course—as generations came and went —the noise built up again: nagging and squabbling and cheering.

"*Silence their caterwauling!*" yelled Enlil out of the windows of Heaven. "Send Drought and Famine! Perhaps when they are dead of thirst and starvation these humans will finally be quiet!"

Well, Ea did as he was told, but hurried ahead, to warn the people of Earth. Once again the cities fell silent. Once again, Enlil relented and Drought and Famine withdrew.

But as time passed, of course, the noise built up again: wars and fairs, circuses and parades, building sites and forges.

Enlil slammed shut the windows of Heaven, but it hardly made a difference.

"I WILL NOT HAVE THIS DIN! DROWN THE WHOLE PACK OF THEM!" he bawled. And this time he summoned all his brother and sister gods and made them all consent to the destruction of Mankind. "And this time, not a word to a soul: not a single soul. Agreed?"

Shamash bowed his head in consent.

Anu grunted and put his fingers in his ears.

Even Nurgal, who had shaped Mankind, agreed.

Even Ishtar, goddess of Love.

Ea, too, gave his consent, though in his heart he was trying to think of some way to rescue the situation. There might just be time to deliver a single message . . .

Utnapishtim broke off from his story. "Seven generations ago, Shurrupak was my city. I was king there. The god Ea has always been esteemed highly in Shurrupak, for his gentleness towards Mankind, and I venture to think that he and I were on good terms. Ea wanted to warn me, but because of his vow could not speak to me directly.

"So he whispered into the *fabric of my house*, do you see?
—the reeds of which its walls were made.

'Reed house! Reed house! Listen and pray!
Would that your walls were torn down today
And from your reeds were built, a craft:
A huge, pitch-covered, roofed-in raft
As tall as she's long as she's wide and square
That those who board her might then be spared
The doom the gods have ordained for Mankind
A Flood which once come will leave nothing behind.
Do not sleep! Keep watch! Keep awake,
Or the thread of life will forever break!'

"That night, when the wind blew on my house, the reeds whispered Ea's words to me as I slept, and I dreamed what I had to do: save all of Nature from Enlil's damnation.

"I told the people of Shurrupak that I had been summoned to sail down to the Underworld, to pay for my sins, and that's why I was building a boat. How could I tell them the truth? Workmen were easy enough to come by, as well. I just offered unlimited supplies of roast meat and rough wine. In a week, I had a boat.

"It had seven decks in all, each one divided into nine sections by bulkheads—to keep the various animals apart. You can't put gazelles in with lions—I mean, you couldn't in those days. I made the reeds watertight with a mixture of melted pitch, oil, and asphalt. It was big—unimaginably big. It covered an acre of ground, and each side of the deck was 120 cubits long—a cube, in fact. Not a seaworthy shape. Not an easy shape to launch. We had to keep shifting the ballast about until she would float two-thirds underwater, stable enough not to turn turtle.

72

"I loaded aboard my family, my animals. I took one male and one female of every species, so that afterwards—after the catastrophe—they would be able to reproduce and replenish the Earth. I mean, what would the Earth be without its animals and birds? In the evening, the rain began. Never seen weather like it. It turned the ground to slurry in an instant. So I went aboard myself, slithering and sliding on the mud slick round the boat, climbing the scaffolding and battened down the last open hatch over my head. It was dark—only the hissing of the rain on the reeds and tar, as if all the waterfalls of Heaven were falling on our heads. But that was nothing.

"At dawn the Lord of the Storm summoned up a black cloud that smothered the whole plain of Shullar and Hanish. Water seemed to well up from the ground—from the abyss under the Earth; the goddess of the underworld smashed all her dams and let it come fountaining up. The seven judges of hell came roaming through the land, torches held aloft, so that the sky outside was permanently lit by an eerie flicker—great rods of lightning wedged between Heaven and Earth.

"That storm smashed the land, like a cup. The boat was soon riding floodwaters through city and plain and forest. I had to stay at my tiller every moment, or we could have foundered against a drowning palace or snagged on the branches of some tree. I couldn't afford to sleep. I could see now why Ea had forbidden me to sleep. For a whole day the storm trampled the world. You could hear people calling out, unable to find one another for the walls of rain. As the rain beat on them, they all began to turn back to clay—to the substance they were made from . . . And how can you sleep while that happens?

73

"Even the gods were afraid. They climbed up to the highest chambers of Heaven, the floodwaters cornering them like cringing dogs against the walls. You could hear the goddess Ishtar howling with remorse, because she had gone along with Enlil's damnation of Mankind. '*Aren't they my people? Didn't I help to give them life? Now look at them—floating in the ocean like so much fish-spawn!*' She wasn't alone in grieving. All the great gods of heaven and hell put their hands over their mouths and wept at what they had done.

"For six days and nights the storm went on. And not for one moment did I close my eyes or sleep. Even when every animal and every child and every star seemed to be asleep, I stayed awake, my hand on the tiller, praying for deliverance. When the drumming of the rain finally stopped on the seventh day, I threw open a hatch, and a bolt of sunlight fell in my face like a bale of yellow hay. I looked out from my ark and what did I see?

". . . Nothing. There was nothing to see. Nothing in any direction but water, flat as any rooftop. I don't have to tell you: I sat down and wept. I lay down and cried like a child. The whole of Mankind turned to clay. The whole of Nature reduced to a slick of red dust under countless fathoms of water.

"My head was stuffed with sleep. I was reeling with weariness. I didn't know whether to believe my eyes or not, but it seemed to me that about fourteen leagues away, there was an island. I blinked and bleared at it. Yes! A bare mountain tip was sticking up out of the water. I won't say I steered for it. We were drifting towards it, willy-nilly, and there we wedged. For seven days we sat wedged on that mountaintop, while the flotsam of a lost world drifted by us— dolls, dishes, gates, wheels, bottles . . .

"On the seventh day, I brought a dove up on deck and let her

go. She flew away . . . but clearly there was nowhere for her to perch because she came back. The next day I loosed a swallow. She flew away too, but the land was still drowned, because back she came. On the third day I loosed a raven. She circled slowly, blackly into the sunny sky then flew off. She didn't come back.

"That was when I knew it was safe to open up every hatch, and free the animals from below-decks. They lumbered out past me, leaving behind a litter of feathers and fur and a stench I won't even try to describe. I watched them straying further and further from the ark as the mountainside gradually emerged, steaming, from under the shrinking floodwaters.

"I was easily visible from Heaven, easily picked off if Enlil was still bent on destroying the entire human race. So I took fourteen cauldrons of oil, and set them up on the mountainside—lit fires under them of the sweetest smelling wood I could forage. As the fumes went up from those cauldrons, the whole dome of the sky was filled with the sweetest smell imaginable. The gods were drawn to it, like flies to honey, like shark to blood; they couldn't keep away. Snuffing up the sweet smoke, they came sighing and swimming through the rain-washed air. Last of all came Ishtar—lovely Ishtar—wearing a necklace of jewels that were every color ever given a name—red, amber, yellow, green, blue, indigo and violet. When she saw that the Flood was over, she lifted it off over her head and threw it into the sky, swearing, 'I shall remember these days! By the jewels of my throat, I shall never forget!'

"She had invented the rainbow, you see.

"Enlil came, of course. When he saw my boat—oh!—I thought he would smash it with a single thunderbolt.

'WHAT?' he yelled. 'HAS ONE OF THEM ESCAPED? WHO WARNED HIM?'

"I cowered down under a corner of the ark, with my head between my knees, hands over my ears.

"But then I heard my friend's voice. Ea was speaking up for me —reasoning with Enlil. 'Punish people when they sin, by all means, but don't destroy them utterly! Where would we be without mortals to dig and tend the earth, to press the oil for our sacrifices, to build the temples for our worship? Do you think we'll take up our tools again and labor and sweat? Think again. Why create the Earth at all, if it is only to stand empty like some house on a hill, its doors banging in the wind. *I* didn't tell the man Utnapishtim about the coming of the Flood. He had the wisdom to dream it. For seven days and seven nights he kept awake, steering the ark safely through the waves. Should such a man die?'

"I had crawled out of hiding to listen. When Enlil turned and saw me, it was too late to duck out of sight again, so I stood up. He ordered me and my wife to go aboard the ark. With trembling knees, we went up the gangplank again, and knelt down on the uppermost deck. Up came Enlil, closer and closer, reaching out his hands. Then, just when I thought I would die of fear, he took both Saba and I by the hand and stood between us. He touched our foreheads and said, 'Live forever, man of Shurrupak. Make your home on Paradise Shore, beyond the river of Death. And live forever, as we gods do!'"

9 The bread of sorrow

"Your eyelids are heavy, King of Uruk. How long since you slept?"

Gilgamesh gave a start. "A day. Two days, perhaps . . . If only the gods would test me like that!"

Utnapishtim exchanged a smile with his wife. "No need. I will set you a test. I don't pride myself on what I did—I had no choice, and the gods helped me. But could *you* stay awake seven days and seven nights, if lives depended on it?"

"Of course!" said Gilgamesh, jumping to his feet.

So Gilgamesh stood on Paradise Shore, eyes wide, despite their red rims. What was so hard about defeating sleep, after all? Did it have claws or horns or fangs? Did it come wearing armor? No. Sleep was soft and wool-lined. Sleep came, swirling and silken, rolling over a man like fog.

The sea whispered behind Gilgamesh. The ropes of the hammock creaked in the tree. Gilgamesh sat down again and rested his eyes for a moment. Weary? He had never been weary as a young man. How long ago was that? When was it that that young man had paced about his palace too full of energy to sleep? Not so very long, surely? Was old age already battening on him like a vampire bat, draining him of energy? For a moment, he thought he saw it bearing down on him, and opened his eyes in fright. But it was only the awning flapping, flapping in the sea-whispering breeze . . .

"Wife," said Utnapishtim, as Gilgamesh slumped sideways into the soundest of sleeps. "Go and cook a loaf and set it down by our guest for him to eat when he wakes."

"He won't wake for a week, poor weary soul," said Saba.

"I know that," said Utnapishtim. "But bake it anyway."

Every morning, Saba baked a loaf of bread and set it by Gilgamesh where he slept on the seashore. They lay like seven pillows beside the sleeping King of Uruk.

When at last he stirred, his opening eyes struggled to focus. The next moment he was on his feet, swaying slightly with dizziness.

"That was a great sleep, Gilgamesh," said Utnapishtim. "A great sleep born out of a great weariness."

"Sleep? Me? No, no! I just nodded for a moment. Not asleep. I wasn't asleep!"

"For seven days and seven nights you slept, my friend."

"Never! What do you take me for, a fool?"

"Each day I had my wife bake a loaf. Look. There they are.

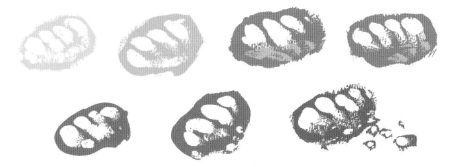

You can see how old they are. The first is green with mold, the last is still warm. In between are all the stages a loaf goes through before it ceases to be a loaf. A little like the life of man, wouldn't you say? Sweet smelling and softly tender at first. Harder with age. A harder outer crust to defend a man against life's knocks. Little by little more and more brittle. Then at last—decay. Which loaf of bread are you, I wonder?"

Gilgamesh's reply was to kick the oldest and most mildewed loaf out to sea. It exploded into dust around his foot. He had failed the challenge. His weary, aging body had let him down. He had failed, and failure was a very bitter bread indeed for a man like Gilgamesh to eat.

"Sit down. Breakfast, my friend," said Utnapishtim. "My wife bakes very good bread, and what more does a man need to be happy than a loaf of bread, a jug of wine, and good company? Give up your quest. The gods never meant you to live forever, so why spoil the life they did give you? Is the rainbow any less beautiful because it's short-lived? Or because you can't grasp hold of it? Consider, man. Perhaps it is beautiful expressly *because* of that."

But Gilgamesh was not listening. His heart had turned to mold like that first-made loaf.

All his dreams had exploded into dust. He knelt in the sand and wept, banging his forehead on the ground, tasting his own salt tears run in at the corners of his mouth like spray from the River of Death.

Urshanabi had brought his ferry close in to the beach to see if he could glimpse Gilgamesh. The Faraway was angry. "*Ferryman, you were wrong to bring this man here. Take him away, and take yourself off, too!* Have you not broken your promise to Shamash by bringing him here? You have forfeited your right to sail in the service of the immortals!"

Urshanabi meekly bowed his head in apology, accepting his banishment from Paradise Shore. He helped Gilgamesh aboard and put out to sea again. The mast was mended now: a new sail caught the warm wind. Gilgamesh sat huddled in the stern, still weeping.

"I feel so sorry for the man," said Saba standing in the circle of her husband's arm. "He is so very, very afraid. My heart bleeds for him."

Overhearing her words, Gilgamesh shuddered with shame.

"Am I a god? Could I have granted him immortality?" her husband asked in reply.

"You could have told him about Old-man-young. It's not immortality, but it would have been something. Something, in return for all his sufferings."

Utnapishtim shook his head. "Already he has exhausted his youth and strength on this foolish quest. It would be too great an ordeal—too terrible. I like him too much . . . *You!*"

"*Too much for what? Who is Old-made-young?*" Gilgamesh, hearing the conversation, had grabbed the helm out of Urshanabi's hands, turned the boat about and run it ashore again.

81

Now he had hold of Utnapishtim. "What did she mean? *Tell me!*"

"Old-man-young! Old-man-young!" cried Utnapishtim. "Calmly, man! Put me down! It is the name of a plant! Must you go looking for disappointment even at the bottom of the sea?"

"*Is that where it grows? What does it look like? What does it do? How will I find it? Tell me! Tell me everything!*"

And so Utnapishtim told Gilgamesh about Old-man-young: a single weed growing off-shore, protected by ripping currents and armed with thorns so sharp that even the crabs could not slice it through with their armoured claws. "Grip it tight and fetch it up to the light, and it has magic enough to make a hundred old men young again," said Utnapishtim.

But whereas there had been friendship in his eyes before, there was a faraway look now, a saddened vexation at Gilgamesh's lack of manners, gratitude, and kingly dignity.

10 The Plant of Life

"I shan't use it first myself," Gilgamesh told the ferryman. He sat on the sluice-gates tying rocks to his ankles with cords from the ferry's rigging. "I shall give it to the old men of Uruk, and see them grow young again before my eyes.

Imagine! All the wisdom of old age in the body of a young man! Uruk will be the greatest city on all the plains of the world!" The rocks scraped the skin from his anklebones, but he barely noticed, so intent was he on finding the prickly plant.

At the mouth of the nearby river stood a reservoir of fresh water. "You must lift the sluice-gate and let the out-rush of water carry you out to sea," said the ferryman. "Those rocks will keep you from bobbing up to the surface too soon."

He would have to hold his breath all the time. He was not a swimming sort of a man, and envied now the little boys he had seen in Uruk leaping into the Euphrates for the sheer fun of it.

The sluice-gates were hard to lift, but suddenly the pent-up water inside was surging out to sea. Filling his lungs so full he felt them bulge through his ribs, Gilgamesh dropped off the gate and into the racing torrent.

The cold clamped round his ribs and forced out half the

air he had breathed in. The current turned him over and over; the rocks tied to his ankles banging about him, bruising his head and body and legs. He no longer knew which way up he was—which way to struggle for air. He opened his clenched eyes and saw only the swirling sand and the bubbles jarred from his own nose and mouth.

He peered ahead, hand clapped over nose and mouth, trying to keep the air in his chest. Gradually the water became clear, the current behind him weakening. Then the tide rip struck him like a battering ram.

And there it was, on the seabed—a dark green snaggle of leaves and spiky stalks. Not another plant grew in the strong current—only this plant was too well rooted to be dislodged.

He would have only one chance. If he failed to grasp the plant, he would be swept on by and lose it forever. He scuffed his feet, elbows, knees against the seabed in an attempt to slow down, then reached out and grabbed the plant with both fists.

It was nettle and briar and cactus in one. The pain was so intense that he thought the plant must be on fire, his hands burning. He opened his mouth to yell, and the sea rushed in.

But he did not let go.

He fumbled left-handed at the knots tying the rocks to his ankles; they were swollen, impacted, and would not undo. They would hold him down below water, while the breath in his lungs dissolved and he drowned. High above him, the sunny surface was a myriad golden gules shimmering and shoaling. He picked up one of the rocks and sliced at the rope with it, all the while holding fast to the fabulous plant with its bristles and spines and venomous hairs. His lungs flattened inside him like goatskin flagons emptied of wine. Blackness ringed his vision. If he let go, he might yet live.

Then one foot was free, and the loop of the second was slipping over his heel. He set both feet to the seabed, pushed with all his might, and wrenched the plant out of the ocean floor.

He was not sure how he reached the surface. His whole head, his very lungs, seemed to be filled with sea water. And yet he burst through, brandishing the plant high above his head.

Choking and spluttering, he instantly began to kick his legs, and drag the water aside with his left hand. But his right kept tight hold of the blazing agony, the precious weed that would restore his youth and the youth of all the old men of Uruk. His sense of triumph was immense. Not since Enkidu fought at his side, not since the Bull of Heaven had crashed to earth at his feet had Gilgamesh felt a joy like it. Like red hot needles, the plant's bristling spines pierced and cut his palm, but he could bear any amount of pain. The fear which had cramped in his stomach ever since Enkidu's death was gone at last. Not immortal, perhaps, but young again and full of vigor, Gilgamesh would soon feel Life course through him like meltwater down a dried up river bed. He would have time and strength enough to do such deeds as would make the gods relent and say, "Look! Look at this Gilgamesh! Shall such a man die? Never!"

Gilgamesh trod water. The waves shouldered and shoved him. He could not see the shore. He had used up all his strength in picking the plant. What if the current was sweeping him out to sea?

What if it washed him out as far as the River of Death. What good would the plant be to him then?

Then he rolled over . . . and to his inexpressible joy saw a snake-headed prow rearing up out of a golden bow-wave.

As Urshanabi pulled him aboard, Gilgamesh prattled and babbled like a little boy. He whirled Urshanabi about in a wild, wet dance, and Urshanabi laughed and struggled, nodded and danced. He had grown fond of the impetuous King of Uruk.

Suddenly Gilgamesh wanted very much to be home in Uruk—to tell his mother, to see his shady rooms again, to know how the rebuilding work was progressing. He should not have left his people in time of drought. Was that any way for the father of his people to behave? Suddenly he stopped dancing. "Urshanabi! What have I done to you! I've robbed you of your livelihood! I've put you out of favor with the gods!"

Urshanabi shrugged.

"Come home with me, Urshanabi! Come back to Uruk. The Euphrates is no sea, but at least the spray of it can't kill you. Come with me. There's no place in the world like Uruk!"

As the two men sailed back over the ocean, the sea water dried on Gilgamesh and left him salt-caked and uncomfortable. Brown blood caked his hands and arms from where he had grasped the plant, and his hair was seeded with saltwater prawns. He felt less like a king than a sardine drying in the sun. After they had walked thirty leagues, he spotted a deep cool lake and decided to bathe.

He set the plant down on a flat rock, and immersed himself in the cool water. His grey hair spread out around his face as he floated on his back, looking up at the sky.

Soon he would be wearing linen again and eating stoned olives and taking a glass of wine on the sill of his room in the Uruk palace. He would offer up sacrifices, making things right with the gods. He would ask their blessing on the people of his city, then summon the masons to carve this latest adventure on the bare wall—the fights, the victories, the achievements. He would give Urshanabi some post in government as compensation for what he had lost. "Poor man! To think I caused his banishment." He thought of Siduri, the wine-seller on the seashore, and how pleased she had been when he called on his return journey to show her the plant. Even so, she had repeated her advice. "Take a wife. You think this bit of greenery makes you happy? It's nothing in comparison with a child."

The cool clean water crept in at his ears and the corners of his mouth and eyes. He was very happy. There were good people in the world—more than he had thought.

Glancing towards the rock, he saw the green plant—a tatter of thorns and spines. He saw the snake, too—of no great size: just a common snake. It slithered out of a crevice, tasting a peculiar scent on the air with its quivering forked tongue.

"*NO!*"

It crossed the rock in a twinkling, unhinged its jaws and swallowed the plant, insensitive to pain.

"*NO! NO! NO!*"

At once, its dull mantle of scales split from end to end, and a new snake emerged, shining and brightly colored. Then it was gone, leaving behind the transparent husk of its sloughed skin, leaving behind its old age.

Not a stem, not a leaf, not a bristle or a thorn remained of the plant called Old-man-young. And all its magic—every twinkle and shimmer—was gone too, down into the snake's belly.

11 Home

Gilgamesh knelt on the bank of the pool vomiting his misery in great retching sobs. He beat his torn fists on the ground and howled like a wild animal.

"All gone, Urshanabi! What was it all for? All those weeks! All that suffering and pain! What am I? Nobody! Some sick old man with nothing to show for it but tears!"

"Oh, I wouldn't say—" Urshanabi murmured comfort, but Gilgamesh was deaf to anything but his own lament.

They traveled back through the Garden of the Gods, gathering up gemstones like so many fallen petals from under the flower bushes. They stumbled back through the Mashu Mountain: somehow it was not so dark for two. Besides, the darkness inside Gilgamesh was ten times as black.

They traveled back through the Gates of Shamash, where the Scorpionguards stared at them in astonishment.

They traveled back through the mountain pass where the lions had prowled. There seemed to be just as many as before. But now Gilgamesh was startled by their beauty. Their hides suited them better than they had him. He did not want to slaughter them; they would be soon enough dead, bereft of their lithe, elegant beauty.

"Tell me about Uruk," said Urshanabi, and Gilgamesh found he was eager to do so.

"The city is one part field, one part town, one part gardens. Then there are the temples, of course—wonders of the world! The water from the river is ducted through the city—threads of silver everywhere, like wire in a tapestry. The wall is high and curved. The foundations were laid in the days of the Seven Sages. Even when the Bull of Heaven stamped, those walls stayed standing!"

Urshanabi listened without interrupting.

"My builders are the best. My masons take pride in their work, and my gardeners are skilled at grafting and pruning . . ."

"I wonder you ever left such a place," Urshanabi remarked mildly.

So too did Gilgamesh, when he saw Uruk. Each familiar roof and tower and window was like the features of a well-loved face. The perfumes of his childhood came to the gate to meet him. At least he had lived to see it all again.

As he walked though the streets, people idly looked up at these two grubby strangers. A murmur of excitement built up in their wake. "Can it be?"

"It can't be!"

"The King, you mean? Never! He's long dead, surely!"

"Come and see! Go and tell the children!"

"Look! Look! Gilgamesh the Mighty has come home!"

"Where are the banners?"

"See how white his hair . . ."

"Where has he been?"

An inexpressible tenderness filled Gilgamesh. After being in lonely, distant places, it was good to see so many familiar faces. After the brown of the stony wilderness, the black of the mountain's interior, he wondered at the multicolors of the city. He had forgotten how many flowers there were, how the awnings and drying washing added to the gold of masonry, the red of the terracotta. He had forgotten all the noises, too—women singing, dogs barking, chickens cackling, donkeys braying, the vendors shouting their wares. Only the sound of building had fallen quiet, with no one to order new towers or temples.

A woman's voice drifted from a window. ". . . worst news I've heard. Must we go back now to war and work?" She came to her window and looked out—straight into the face of the King. Her eyes, already fearful, widened into terror as she realized he had heard her. She feared for her life.

Gilgamesh returned her a smile—an awkward, grimacing smile, realizing how rarely he had ever smiled before.

At his shoulder, the ferryman stood gazing about him.

"Well, Urshanabi? Didn't I say it was the finest city in the world?"

Urshanabi smiled and nodded. At last Gilgamesh's tour of the city brought them to the carved friezes depicting the deeds of past heroes. There was Utnapishtim, his odd cube-shaped ark wedged on a mountain top. There were the Seven Sages . . . And there were Enkidu and Gilgamesh bringing home the tallest tree from the Cedar Forest to build new gates for Uruk.

"And this, I take it, is Enkidu," said the ferryman.

Gilgamesh had left Uruk before the scene was carved. At first he could not bear to look. Then he could not stop looking. His hand reached out towards the figure carved high up, far larger than life, in bas-relief. His fingers came to rest on the ankle of Enkidu. "I came back, friend. Just as I was, but I came back." Urshanabi saw that his eyes were full of tears.

The ferryman smiled and shook his head. Nothing could be further from the truth.

12 The Twelfth Tablet

*The skies over Uruk were smoky as the King's sacrifices burned—
meat and fruit, oil and flowers. The gods were drawn like flies to
circle in the perfumed air.*

After fulfilling his duty to the gods, Gilgamesh sent for his masons.
The people groaned. Now the building would begin again; soon it
would be the wars.

But Gilgamesh was too weary for battle campaigns. Since
destroying the steering gear of the ferryboat, he thought twice
about destroying things. Fearing Death, he no longer wished it on
the young men of his city. Exhausted, he no longer wanted anyone
to work themselves into an early grave. He did not want anyone to
mourn, as he had mourned for Enkidu. He looked at the old men
and felt responsible for their frailty.

But he did send for his masons and scribes.

He told them to carve his adventures on the wall of heroes, and
write them on clay tablets for future generations to read. While he
told them his story, they listened like children at his feet, open-
mouthed, fingers in their hair, astounded. They ran home and told
their wives and children, and soon the city buzzed with voices
retelling the epic of Gilgamesh. What a story it was!

The King's dreams re-enacted his adventures. Sometimes he woke crying, sometimes screaming. And sometimes he even woke up laughing.

Through his window he heard the people say, "He has changed! How he has changed!" But how could that be? He had not gained immortality. He had not eaten the prickly plant. Surely it was *they* who had changed. Once they had hated him, and now, for some reason, they loved him.

When the frieze was finished, he went to look at it. "But tell me —why this empty panel at the end? Do you think I will be going on more journeys?" asked Gilgamesh wryly.

"No, sire. But begging your pardon, sire, that panel is to show your funeral . . ."

Gilgamesh rocked as if he had been struck. He returned to the palace and asked to see what his scribe poets had written. They brought him eleven tablets.

"I suppose you realize this is incomplete?" he said, his voice harsh and rasping. "You have not recounted my death."

The scribes bowed low. "Naturally, there will be a *twelfth* tablet, my lord King."

At last, Gilgamesh took to heart the advice of Siduri the wine seller. He did marry, and he did have children. On the day his first son was born, he took the child in his arms and stood on the broad sill of his room overlooking a Uruk golden in the evening sun. Tears ran down his cheeks now as freely as the day his friend had died.

But today he was crying tears of joy.

93

For was he not holding new life in his arms, and did it not have his eyes and his hands and his long feet and his Sumerian nose? Was he not as immortal now as every other father of sons? The child's hand within his own was as small as the seed of a cedar tree.

He called the child Prince Enkidu.

Out of the darkness of sleep a dream hurtled down—a meteor trailing a tail of light, and an axe lying in the street. The meteor was fame, the axe his fate. They were heavy to carry, but no one else would have even tried to pick them up. As it was, Gilgamesh did such things, dared so much, learned such wisdom, conquered such fear that his name outlived the gods themselves.

Long after Enlil and Anu, Ishtar, Ea and Shamash had been forgotten on the Plain-of-Two-Rivers, the fame of Gilgamesh lived on. He was Gilgamesh the Mortal, Gilgamesh the Friend, Gilgamesh the Father, Gilgamesh the Hero, Gilgamesh the Coward, Gilgamesh the Wise Man, Gilgamesh the Fool. Everyone wants to leave their mark on the world, and he left a mark as big as a meteor crashing to earth.

As they carved on the twelfth tablet: *He walked through darkness and so glimpsed the light.*

95

Text copyright © Geraldine McCaughrean 2002
Illustrations copyright © David Parkins 2002

The moral rights of the author and artist have been asserted

Published jointly 2003

in the United Kingdom by
Oxford University Press
Great Clarendon Street, Oxford OX2 6DP U.K.
and the United States of America by
Eerdmans Books for Young Readers
an imprint of
Wm. B. Eerdmans Publishing Co.
255 Jefferson Ave. S.E., Grand Rapids, Michigan 49503

Printed in China

09 08 07 06 05 04   7 6 5 4 3 2

Library of Congress Cataloging-in-Publication Data

McCaughrean, Geraldine.
Gilgamesh the hero / written by Geraldine McCaughrean ;
illustrated by David Parkins.
p. cm.
Summary: A retelling, based on seventh-century B.C. Assyrian clay
tablets, of the wanderings and adventures of the god king, Gilgamesh,
who ruled in ancient Mesopotamia (now Iraq) in about 2700 B.C., and of
his faithful companion, Enkidu.

ISBN 0-8028-5262-9 (hardcover : alk. paper)

1. Gilgamesh--Adaptations. [1. Gilgamesh. 2. Folklore--Iraq.] I.
Parkins, David, ill. II. Title.
PZ8.1.M144Gi 2003
398.2'09567'02--dc21
2003001086

Cover design by Matthew Van Zomeren